CASSIE MINT

A Night to Remember

The Complete Series

BLACK CHERRY
PUBLISHING

Contents

III   Tangling with the Boss

I

Dancing with the Enemy

Description

　　⚜

He's my arch nemesis. The bane of my life.
And I spend the night in his arms...

Jude Jenkins lives for one thing only: driving me up the wall. We work on opposite desks, glaring at each other the whole time. He's the devil. I wouldn't trust him to put me out if I was on fire.

But our rooftop work party changes everything. When we dance... it feels like coming home.

We're still bickering.

But we're inching closer, too.

Maybe this tingly feeling isn't hate after all...

Violet

◦◦◦◦◦

The office is quiet this morning, with the soft purr of phones and shuffle of papers. Mouses click and keyboards tap. Voices murmur over by the water cooler, and my stomach grumbles behind my desk, complaining that half a stale bagel was barely any breakfast at all.

It's never this freaking quiet at Grapevine. Usually, people are laughing on the phone, charming clients and promising the world; flirting by the photocopier and smacking staplers like they're banging a drum. Most days I work with earbuds wedged in my ears, listening to the calming throb of LoFi so I don't snap a pencil and yell at everyone to shut the hell up.

Today is different. Eerily so. But I guess it's the calm before the storm—the hush before tonight's big party.

The air changes in the room as a new pair of footsteps enter behind me. Studiously gnawing on my pencil, I pretend not to notice the way the little hairs on my arms stand on end, nor how my stomach squirms for a whole new reason.

He's here.

Jude Jenkins is here.

It's fine. Of course he's here.

He *works* here, and even though I hate every single thing about this man, even though he is the bane of my life, it shouldn't shock my system every time he walks into a room.

"Violet," Jude says, ruffling my hair as he walks past. My rival throws himself down into the chair opposite mine, then scoots closer to his desk, grinning the whole time. He's in a white shirt with a skinny black tie today, the sleeves rolled to his elbows, and his dark hair is windswept. He looks like a sexy weatherman. Did he go out for a walk? Where?

I glare back from beneath my messed up bangs. "Judas."

He was gone for thirty minutes, but it felt like a week.

"It's just Jude, actually." He tosses a nut and catches it in his mouth, cracking it between his teeth. Dark blue eyes twinkle at me. Why doesn't he ever miss his mouth? He's always so freaking smooth with everything. Does he rehearse that nut trick at home? "But don't feel bad. The pressure of work can get to anybody. Let me know if I should take a few clients off your plate, okay?"

Ugh.

I hate him so much.

My heart's thumping harder already, pulsing with loathing, racing the way it always does when Jude is near. But I force my grip to stay loose around my pencil, because there's no point white-knuckling the stationery where my rival can see, because then he'll *know* he's getting to me.

And Jude Jenkins lives to push my buttons.

Just like I live to push his.

So my smile is slow and smug. I tilt my head, watching him

back, like I'm not bothered at all by my ruffled hair or the explosion of chaos that is his desk; like the sight of his toned forearms does nothing to me. All around us, our coworkers bustle between desks and sip from coffee mugs. It smells like carpet cleaner and warm paper in here.

"That's sweet of you to offer," I say. "But didn't you lose the Pretzel Media contract last month?"

Irritation flashes in those indigo eyes, right before Jude smooths it away with another sunny smile. Still, he can't hide from me.

This is why we've fought tooth and nail since our first day on the job together. This is why we can't leave this *thing* between us the hell alone: we *see* each other.

It's agonizing.

"They went in another direction," Jude says airily, blunt fingers tapping on the only clear patch of his desk. There could be rodents living in that mound of office supplies for all we know. A whole tiny civilization, with a network of tunnels through the bedrock of printouts and binder files. "A *cheaper* direction. If Pretzel can't afford quality, that's hardly my problem, is it Violet? Or would you have halved your fee for them?" He winces with pity, shaking his head. "There's no need to be desperate. Know your worth! Your last video was almost good."

My last video was fucking *awesome*, and this jerk knows it. It was a music video for an up-and-coming pop star, one we filmed on location in all these abandoned jungly warehouses, and it went so well that the office held a little screening so the interns could take notes. So nyuh.

Jude's just being an ass. Like always.

"Your desk is a disaster zone." Spinning my pencil around,

I poke the eraser into a pile of notepads and opened letters, shunting them back across the boundary line between our desks. A paper clip drops to the floor, pinging across the polished floorboards. The whole pile trembles. "I should call pest control. Do you live like this at home? Are you in Hoarders Anonymous?"

Jude leans forward, his voice dropping low—and every word rumbles through me, tingling in the marrow of my bones as he says, "Always so curious about my home life. If you want to see my apartment, Violet, you only need to ask."

Damn the heat creeping into my cheeks. Damn this urge to fan my face. This always happens: Jude saunters over and pushes all my buttons, one by one, until I don't know whether I want to strangle him or crawl into his lap.

He's always teasing me. *Mocking* me, with one sardonic eyebrow raised, hungry eyes boring into mine. Silently challenging me to bite back.

And I do like sparring. But what would it be like to have Jude's praise for once? To lay down our weapons? To take his plush bottom lip between my teeth and gently pull?

Someone wrestles a window open on the other side of the room, and a fresh breeze barges inside, ruffling everyone's papers on their desks.

I raise one eyebrow, determined not to seem flustered, even as a tiny, traitorous part of me wants to call Jude's bluff. Wants to ask for an invite to Jenkins HQ after all, and see what might come of it.

Because *of course* I want to see this handsome jerk in his natural habitat, and find out which color he paints his walls. See what art he hangs, if any, and which brand of coffee he drinks, and whether he'd still tease me like this if we were alone.

Would I want him to? I think so.

But maybe I'm giving him too much credit. Judging by the landslide of crap on his desk, Jude must live on a trash heap out by the city limits. He probably collects rainwater in a barrel to shave, and hangs his clothes out to dry on a broken stepladder. Probably gazes into his own beautiful, evil eyes using a scratched old hubcap.

"So tonight's the night," he says now, tapping on his keyboard and bringing his monitor to life, logging in with a blur of fingers. It's so unfair that this man looks good in the electrical glow—healthy and clear-skinned, with sharp cheekbones and bright eyes. No wonder I hate him. Why can't he look sickly and tired like everyone else? It's plain rude.

"Hm?" Tonight?

"The rooftop party," Jude says, enunciating each word as he glances over at me. "The Grapevine ten year anniversary thing. You do work here, right? You didn't just wander in from the street like a raccoon?"

My phone buzzes and I ignore him, tapping on the screen and frowning at my latest email like it's super important. Anything to avoid that electric gaze.

"More pizza coupons?"

Falafel, actually. God, I hate this man.

"Excuse me, please." Scooping up my phone, I stand quickly and tug my dress straight. "I need to make a very urgent call."

"Get me dough balls!" Jude yells after me, breaking the spell of quiet that settled over the office all morning. Suddenly, phones are ringing and desk drawers are slamming, and someone starts blasting music through their headphones. The calm is over.

I power walk all the way to the elevator, and don't breathe properly until the doors swoop shut. My cheeks are pink in the mirrored walls, and my dark hair is a mess thanks to *someone*. My pulse taps visibly in my throat.

But once I'm alone, where no one else can see, I allow myself a reluctant smile.

Dough balls. Such an ass.

Jude

~∽◦∽◦∽~

I slump in my chair once Violet is gone, leftover adrenaline turning my muscles to lead. My heart's working extra hard right now, pounding away against my ribs, and my mouth is dry. Swigging from my water bottle, I watch the sign above the elevator count down the floors.

Where is that little harpy going? Who messaged her?

And will she be at the party tonight? Because there's no point in going if Violet won't be there.

No offense to the rest of the people working at Grapevine, but there's only one person in this whole office who makes me feel alive, and that's my snarky little rival. If she's not coming, I might as well go to my usual Friday night basketball game. Try to sweat out this constant, gnawing frustration I build up each week working opposite Violet Moore.

Hmm. What to do? A mouse pad flops to the floor as I pick up my work phone, dialing the extension for the boss's assistant. Chair creaking, I snatch up the mouse pad and stuff it in an overfull drawer.

One ring.

Two.

Maybe I have gone overboard with the mess. It's becoming a Healthy and Safety hazard, but I can't back down from Violet. Can't let her think she's won by huffing at me through those pouty red lips. I only started piling up the mess at all because she rolled her eyes at my stack of mail that one time, and now look at me. One day there will be an avalanche, and I'll die here, buried in post-its. Snuffed out by my need to make Violet scoff.

Will she mourn for me? Will she wear all black like a widow, and refuse to spar with anybody else? Hope so.

"Hello!" The boss's assistant, Hazel, sounds as chipper as ever down the phone, even though she works for the grumpiest man in the city. "Jude, isn't it? Can I help with something?"

"Yeeees." Scratching my chin, I wince at the water cooler against the far wall, because there's no way around it. This is going to sound weird. "Do you have a guest list for tonight? Do you know who's planning to attend?"

"Of course!" Hazel's positivity beams down the phone, scorching my ear, and fuck—for a split second, I really miss Violet's quiet sarcasm. "There will be food and an open bar, so of course I have the numbers. Oh, wait a second—"

There's a muffled thump. A very sunshiney curse. Fingers tap on a keyboard, then a triumphant puff of breath crackles through the line.

"Yes! Here we go. There are seventy three confirmed attendees for tonight."

Uh-huh. And seventy two of them don't interest me at all.

"Great. Is Violet Moore on that list?"

Hazel hums, whispering names under her breath as she scans.

How the hell that woman stays so cheerful working for Mr Corbin, I'll never know—and how *he* tolerates her plucky innocence is a mystery. I once saw him glare at a puppy on the sidewalk outside.

"Violet Moore," Hazel says. "Violet Moore…"

My abs clench as I wait.

This is eternal.

"Here she is!" Hazel says at last, and my shoulders drop down from my ears. So Violet *is* going tonight, that minx. And if she'll be there, so will I. "Remind her that we'll be running a car service at the end of the night, won't you?"

"Gladly." Thanking Hazel and hanging up, I spin to face Violet's empty chair, an evil smile spreading over my face.

Violet Moore, at a party.

Violet Moore, after hours.

What will she wear? What's her drink of choice? Will she lash me with her usual insults, or will she soften up away from the office? I'm not sure which I'd prefer.

All I know is: I will *definitely* be there to find out.

* * *

Violet returns from her mystery errand after twenty minutes, with her dark bangs neatened and her red lipstick reapplied. She's wearing an olive green shirt dress and cowboy boots today, and every stride she takes across the office sends the fabric swishing around her thighs.

"Judas."

Violet nods at me once before dropping into her chair. Unlike mine, Violet's desk is obsessively tidy, with everything except her mouse, keyboard, and pencil cup kept tucked out of sight in her drawers. I happen to know she keeps cleaning wipes in there too, scrubbing the desk when she thinks I'm not looking. She's right, I'd mock her for it.

Bet her apartment is an empty white cube with no visible possessions. Bet her favorite playlist is nothing but static, and her perfume is a spritz of cleaning spray.

"I missed you," I say.

Violet rolls her eyes, logging into her computer. She's going to ignore me, then; going to be the bigger person. That's fine. Now that I know she'll be at the party tonight, I'm all warm and relaxed inside, feeling extra magnanimous. The phones chirping all around us sound like birds tweeting, and the steady rattle of the copier's paper tray is like waves crashing on the shore.

Violet is back, and this is paradise.

"I sent you some notes on that adventure tour company proposal. For the campaign idea you pitched on Tuesday? They're in your inbox." The breeze gusts through the office again, ruffling the mound of crap on my desk until it wobbles.

Violet's red lips press together, her gaze fixed on the screen. "Thank you," she grits out. "But if I need your help, I will ask for it."

I doubt that somehow.

"What are you wearing later?" Should leave her alone, should stop prodding at her, but I can't help myself. Not when she's so adorably scrunchy. "We should coordinate. Make sure we don't show up in the same outfit."

Violet scowls at her monitor, jabbing at her mouse extra hard. She doesn't answer me, but that's fine—we'll have plenty of time for chit-chat tonight.

Violet Moore on a rooftop under the stars.

It's everything I've been waiting for.

Violet

What am I wearing tonight? It sucks that a teasing question from Jude Jenkins, one clearly meant to wind me up and nothing more, haunts me all afternoon. Because I had an outfit in mind for tonight—a silk wrap dress in a misty lavender color, a secret gem that I found in a thrift store last month. But now that he's asked about it, I'm second guessing everything. Wondering whether *Jude Jenkins*, of all people, will like that dress.

Whether he'd like to touch it, grazing his fingertips over the silk.

Whether he'll picture the dress puddled on his bedroom floor.

Gah. Kill me now.

By 3pm, I've made an angry little list in my spiral notebook, all outfit ideas for tonight. Nothing feels right, my whole closet is useless, and I can't focus on my *actual* work.

I should be brainstorming ideas for that electric car commercial, not wondering how Jude feels about side-boob. If my rival ever discovers this crush, he will tear me to shreds.

As the day wears on, the office gets buzzier. Louder. Everyone's restless and impatient, willing the hours away, already gossiping about tonight. Laying bets on who will sneak away to hook up; who'll turn up three hours late and half-buzzed; whether Mr Corbin will ever crack a smile. On days like these, there's only one pocket of calm in this whole company, and that's at my friend Lucy's desk in the Accounts department.

My boots thud against the stairwell steps as I climb, my dress swishing around my legs. Would have been quicker to take the elevator, but I need to burn off some of this antsy energy.

Lucy will know what to do. She'll say all the right things, and she'll look at me with endless patience, just like she always does. Yeah.

The Accounts department is equally jittery and loud when I push through the doors, and I hunt down Lucy at her desk in the corner. She's wearing a huge, boxy pair of noise-canceling headphones, tapping a pen against the frame of her glasses as she stares at her screen.

Spreadsheets. Always spreadsheets.

There are so many printers running on this floor, their hum tickles through my feet.

"Boo." I tap my friend on the shoulder, smirking when she jumps and spins around. Lucy slides her headphones down to her neck, blinking as she drags the spare chair out for me with her ankle. Her body's making room for me before her brain has caught up.

"Hey," she says at last. "Is it manic downstairs too?"

"You bet."

Over her years working here, Lucy has built up a makeshift

wall of potted plants, cutting her cubicle off from the rest of the office. Once I sit down, we're surrounded by foliage, and it smells like green leaves and damp soil. My blood pressure starts to lower.

It's genius, really. If I could barricade Jude Jenkins away with plant life, I would.

"Can't believe you keep all these alive." A leaf shivers when I flick it.

Lucy scoffs gently. "It's not that difficult, Vi."

"Not for you, maybe." Because Lucy is steady, diligent, responsible—an island of calm in the hectic waters of life. When everyone else loses their mind on days like today, she's always plugging along, tapping away at her spreadsheets. Always buttoned up in a cardigan, her auburn hair tied up in a neat bun, glasses polished to a shine.

Meanwhile, I'm ready to howl at the ceiling over Jude Jenkins and the way his teasing gaze makes me feel: ready to burst.

"So what's up?" Lucy asks it nicely, encouraging me with a nod, but her eyes flick to that spreadsheet. I'm interrupting her flow. "Let me guess: Jude Jenkins said or did something and it spun you out."

Yes. Damn it.

And this is not my first visit here this week.

"No," I lie. "I'm wondering what to wear tonight."

Lucy shrugs. "Jude likes you in everything. Don't stress about it."

Gah!

"He does not. And I don't care if he does."

Lucy's smile is teasing. "Sure."

And… that is such bullshit. Jude Jenkins is my *arch rival*, not a flesh and blood man. If he did feel things like that, if he crushed on me back, he'd be positively dangerous with those broad shoulders and those knowing eyes and the slow, teasing smile he gives me sometimes. I'd be a goner. Roadkill.

But he doesn't see me like that; doesn't want me that way. Obviously not. It's deluded. Otherwise why would I be going to this party alone?

Though Jude's words from earlier drift across my mind: *If you want to see my apartment, Violet, you only need to ask.*

A shiver coasts down my limbs, even as I tell myself he didn't mean it. Psychological warfare: that's what everything is with Jude. Nothing can be trusted, *especially* not flirting.

I wish.

I secretly, desperately wish.

"Wear that wrap dress you bought last month." Lucy nods her head, decisive in exactly the way I need. See: this is why I come to her for help. Lucy always saves the day. "The one from that thrift store we liked? You looked amazing in that—like a classic movie star. And who knows?" Her mouth twitches. "Maybe by the end of the night, Jude will unwrap you."

My heart lurches.

"I don't want that." The chair clatters back as I stand, and I nearly tumble into a potted shrub, cheeks flaming. "Oops. Sorry. Thanks, Luce."

"No problem." She's already turning away, fitting those headphones back over her ears. And when I belatedly ask what *she's* wearing tonight, Lucy's ears flush pink but she pretends not to hear me. Her fingers tap away at the keys, plugging in some mysterious formula to her spreadsheet.

That's cool. I'll see her outfit later—and I'll figure out whatever's got my calm bestie squirming with nerves in her seat.

It's going to be a big night.
I can feel it.

* * *

"Jude Jenkins is nothing to you." Hours later, my breath fogs the bathroom mirror in my apartment as I lean close, slicking on my cherry-red lipstick. "Less than nothing. He is a speck of dust in this infinite universe." My lips smack together, and I inspect myself with a frown.

Messy brunette bangs and shoulder-length hair. Gray eyes lined with kohl, and a tiny gold nose stud, and beneath that, the misty lavender wrap dress, clinging to my small curves.

It'll do.

"When Jude looks at you, that squirmy feeling is pure hate. The need to stare at him all the time is because you instinctively know not to trust him." My mouth drops open as I brush mascara over my lashes.

They're not the kind of affirmations you'll find in any self help book, but they've worked for me over the years. Whatever works, right? And sometimes, just sometimes, I need this reminder—that Jude Jenkins is not for me. That the raw, wild energy pulsing between us is pure loathing, and nothing more.

Nothing more.

Forget my stupid crush. Forget the rock-hard body I saw once when he spilled hot coffee and had to whip off his shirt at his desk. Forget the toned chest and ridged abs that are burned into my retinas, and the way my thighs squeezed together beneath the table that day. The way I forgot to breathe.

Not. For. Me.

Besides, what use is a beautiful body when it comes attached to such a terrible personality? And Jude Jenkins has dedicated his life to teasing me; to making me feel cranky and on edge. If he were a drug, I'd be in a twelve step program, trying to quit that man.

Trying to quit playing along.

Quit teasing him back.

Quit *wanting* him like this, in such a restless, needy way—blushing after him in the safety of my apartment, where no one else can see my secret shame.

Might as well name my vibrator 'Jude Junior' at this point, because that jerk rules my hormones and my deepest, most private thoughts.

"He's nothing to you," I say again, fluffing my hair.

Maybe this time, I'll believe it.

Jude

S ay what you will about Leo Corbin, CEO of Grapevine—
he really knows how to throw a party. Or at least his
assistant does, since Hazel has been run ragged for
months planning tonight, always sucking on a giant iced coffee
whenever she hustles past in the office, muttering under her
breath about vendors and invites and canapes.

When I step out onto the skyscraper rooftop, the stars glitter
high above, and Hazel is there, practically vibrating with
excitement by the boss's side. She's in a pink cocktail dress,
her blonde hair tied in a high ponytail, while he looms over
her like a grumpy raven.

Mr Corbin nods at me, expression dour, and pumps my hand.
"Thank you for coming…"

Hazel leans close to him and whispers, "Jude."

"Jude." The boss attempts a small smile, then aborts with a
huff, waving me into the party. "Enjoy."

Stifling a grin, I nudge past and plunge into the crowd as
Hazel's hissed recriminations fade behind me. Only the boss's

21

bubbly assistant ever tells him off, and I would fucking love to eavesdrop—but there's no time tonight. No time to think about anything except one thing.

Violet Moore is here.

She's *near.*

She's somewhere on this rooftop, dressed in evening wear. Sipping a drink, or laughing with that girl from Accounts, or—god forbid—dancing in that press of bodies, twined around some jerk from Legal. Shit. And I've pissed myself off with that last scenario, my strides getting longer and my chest pinching tight, but when I scan the makeshift dance floor... Violet's not there.

Whew.

Okay. Bullet dodged.

Swallowing hard, I tug at my collar and peer around the party, taking it in properly for the first time. The rooftop bustles with bodies, and string lights climb trellises behind three pop-up bars. A live band plays from a small stage, their music upbeat, while guests laugh and chat in small groups and nibble on canapes.

In the center of the roof glows a swimming pool. Steam rises in billowing clouds off the water, and dappled light dances on the surface. Most people are giving the pool a wide berth, treating it like a water feature, but a few guests have already plopped down on the sun loungers for a more casual chat.

So *this* is how Leo Corbin lives. Hazel let it slip once in the break room—that this is *his* building, and the boss lives in the penthouse apartment. It's his private rooftop. Though it's impossible to picture him swimming laps in the pool or stretching out on a sun lounger on a Sunday morning, working through the week's crossword.

It's too human. Surely his grumpy circuits would fry.

"Violet!"

The voice comes from behind me. I wheel around, face already cracking into a grin. But it's not her—of course it's not her, why would Violet call her own name? She's not a fucking Pokemon—it's that girl from Accounts. The quiet, curvy one with the school ma'am glasses. She's clinging to a handsome man's arm, waving across the crowd, hopping from foot-to-foot with excitement.

Can't blame her. That's how I feel whenever I see Violet Moore, too: ready to float up to the ceiling. And—*Christ*, there she is, slipping easily through the press of bodies, draped in mist-colored silk. Violet's lips are red, like always, and her long legs end in strappy heels. A warm smile plays around her mouth as she goes to hug her friend.

"Darius," Violet says when she steps back, nodding at her friend's date. So *that's* why he's familiar—he's Grapevine's star composer. The closest thing our company has to a celebrity. Violet glances between the pair of them, bemused but happy. "I didn't expect... well. Hi. Nice to see you."

The composer slings an arm around his date's shoulder, and the girl from Accounts flushes bright red. "You too."

Violet looks like she has a million questions, like she's ready to drag her friend aside for a gossip fest, but screw it—I've hung back for long enough. Have already exercised extreme patience where my rival is concerned.

It's been hours since we spoke. Hours! I *need* to see her up close.

When I step forward, Violet jolts, the smile dropping off her face.

I don't love that, but the beautiful shiver that coasts through her… that helps soothe the blow. Violet's lips part, and her nostrils flare as she sucks in a deep breath.

"Judas," she greets flatly. Does she even realize that she's leaning toward me? Craning forward like a flower seeking sunshine? The others turn away, greeting someone else.

"Hello Violet."

Already we're drifting away together to a quiet spot, pulled like magnets. Already her pupils are dilating, and she's wetting her lips, and my abs are clenched beneath my dark blue shirt. Every moment with this woman feels like foreplay.

"You look beautiful," I say, and when she blinks in shock, I can't resist adding: "Though there's no need to dress up for me, sweetheart. You could seduce me in a garbage bag."

True, all true.

"Such high standards." Violet rolls her eyes, but she can't hide the pink tinge to her cheeks. She's pleased to see me too. "You should really work on that."

"Oh, I am." Every time I make her blush, or laugh, or roll her eyes, I'm raising the bar. Isn't that obvious?

Violet lets me cup her bare elbow and draw her into my arms, though we're far away from the dance floor. Her body curves against mine and her arms wind around my neck, even as she scowls at me from beneath her bangs. She might hate me, but her body disagrees.

"I'm working incredibly hard," I say.

And it's true: I'm working hard to torment her.

To *win* her.

To make her feel as jumbled up and lost as I do; to make sure I'm not in this alone.

Because it's not fair that I dream about Violet Moore every night while she swans about, living her carefree life. It's not fair that she wrinkles her nose at me, full of contempt, and meanwhile I bite my fist in the shower every morning, choking back her name.

She's stolen my power. Ensnared me with her witchy ways. But *I* know she wants me too. She can't hide from me.

Spreading a palm over her lower back, I press us closer, sealing our bodies together. Violet's heart beats rapidly, knocking against my chest, and she's so soft, so feminine, her scent laced with berries. My stomach growls.

Yes. It's taken us too damn long to come even this far.

"I loathe you," Violet murmurs, though she's gazing up at me through her lashes.

My chest burns. "The feeling is entirely mutual."

"I'm serious," she says, even as her arms wind tighter around my neck; even as she pushes onto her toes, bringing our mouths a single breath apart. "You are the most irritating man I've ever met. I go to sleep every night cursing your name."

"Stop flirting with me."

Our noses brush together, and we're spinning in slow circles—never mind that the band is playing a fast song. Never mind that this is public. Colleagues glance over at us and whisper, and there are a few muffled laughs. We're causing a spectacle, but I don't care.

I *do not* care.

"If you kiss me," I say, "I'll call for HR." Our mouths get closer, almost brushing together, and my heart's booming now, pulse slamming in my ears. Every cell in my body is tense, on edge, urging her to *do it, do it, do it.*

Will she do it? Will she kiss me at last? I'll die if she won't. I'll keel over onto the nearest sun lounger, struck down in my prime.

"If *you* kiss *me*, I'll chew off your tongue," Violet returns, and she's plastered so close I can feel every curve and dip of her body against mine. Could map her with my eyes closed. It's everything I thought it would be: hot and sweet and agonizing.

Despite the turmoil inside my chest, my shrug is casual. "Might be worth the risk. Do I even use my tongue that much?"

Violet snorts. "I *knew* you'd be that kind of guy."

And she's so aggravating, such a shameless little harpy, that I growl as I duck down to nuzzle her ear. I'm squeezing her hips now, hard enough to wrinkle her dress, and I should ease off on her but I can't. We've started something here and I can't stop it, no matter how many of our colleagues keep stealing glances. My body has taken the wheel.

If I step away, I'll break the spell. This will be over too soon, and what if I have to wait years for my next taste?

No. Need to drag this out. Need to commit every detail of this moment to memory: Violet's warm skin, her husky voice, the scent of chlorine from the nearby pool. All of it.

Because she said so herself: this woman loathes me. And who can blame her? Over the last few years, I've made it my personal mission to wind Violet Moore up like a clockwork doll. I've pushed and prodded and teased until she can barely stand five minutes in my presence, and it's all my fault, all my own short-sighted idiocy, but something about this woman short-circuits my brain.

Monkey see, monkey tease.

Monkey fall in unrequited love.

Stupid monkey.

"So you *do* think about us," I murmur. "I knew you did." My thumb strokes her hip bone through the silk of her dress. "Bet you daydream about it all the time. Bet you doodle my name in your neat little planner."

A strangled laugh. "You wish."

I *do* wish.

And I like it here, this close to her perfumed neck, with her dark, glossy hair tickling my nose and her earlobe close enough to nibble. I like that Violet doesn't care about our witnesses either; that she's too wrapped up in this moment to feel self-conscious. Fuck, I like *her*. So, so much. Why can't she see that?

Something twists inside me—something mean and dark and hungry. Something bitter, because I've denied this for too long.

No, *we've* denied this for too long, trading insults when we could have worked out our frustrations in a much more fun way. I'm so tired of sniping when all I want to do is bury my face between those soft thighs.

We've wasted so much precious time together. Why does Violet fight me at every goddamn step of the way? Why can't she listen for once?

Not everything is a joke. When I flirt with her, I *mean* it, damn it.

"Bet you plan your outfits everyday, wondering what will catch my eye." Spiky nerves crackle like embers under my skin—and though I'm speaking softly, some of that bitterness and impatience seeps through. Maybe it's because I've tried telling this woman how I feel so many times, but my teasing words sound all wrong: harsh and judgmental. "Bet you planned this outfit for me. You act so high and mighty, but you'd beg for it, Violet Moore. The moment I got you alone, you'd drop to your knees and beg."

As soon as the words leave my mouth, I know I've misjudged. I've gone too far.

27

Because Violet stiffens against me, her breath freezing in her throat, and when I nudge her with my nose, she makes a strangled noise of pure fury.

"Get. *Away.* From. Me."

I stumble back, bitter cold already gnawing on my bones. My stomach drops. For once, I'm not grinning, not taunting her at all—but Violet doesn't seem to notice that fact. She's too busy glaring at me, scorching me with her unbridled hatred.

My mouth tastes sour with regret. Christ, why did I say that? It sounded hotter in my head; less like an insult. Guess I forgot that we're not *actually* involved the way I want us to be, and I have no business speaking to her like that.

Shit. Shit, shit, shit.

"Violet—"

"I'd rather *die*," she spits, tugging at her dress straight until all my creases are gone. Like we were never pressed together at all, and the last few minutes are nothing but a bad memory. "I'd throw myself off this roof before kissing you, Jude Jenkins. You get that, right? Tell me you get that."

And my insides plummet down, down, down, all the way to street level, but my smile is bland. "Loud and clear."

Because what else is there to say? Violet Moore has won. I want her desperately, I've made that clear in front of everyone, and she'd rather be a pancake on the sidewalk than let this happen.

Violet has spoken: I'm her rival. Nothing more.

Something flickers behind her gray eyes as we hover in silence—uncertainty, maybe. Even regret. The sounds of the party wash over us both, crowding out the painful static buzzing in my brain, and the Legal bros are staring, delighted. Chlorine scents my shaky breaths.

28

Violet softens, her lips parting to speak, but I'm already turning away and plunging back into the crowd. I shoulder my way toward the nearest bar.

She doesn't need to give me the full lecture. Doesn't need to let me down gently.

The only thing between us is hate. Message received.

Violet

O kay, I was way too harsh just then. Crap. Why did I lash out at Jude like that? Why lose my freaking mind? Because sure, he was kind of an ass, but I went full nuclear on him. There's a smoking crater where he just stood.

All I know is we were spinning together, *dancing*, his filthy whispers tickling my ear—and as he held me, happiness and relief sung through my blood. It felt like everything I've been craving for the last few years; like coming home after a long, hard journey. So perfect.

Then... he said *that*.

The thing about me kneeling for him. About me begging. Those words hit me like a blow to the stomach. And I guess they broke something inside me, made me flinch and lash out, but not because I was repulsed. Not at all.

But because it's *true*.

Holy hell.

How many times have I pictured exactly that while laying

in bed at night? Kneeling for my arch rival and begging for a taste? How many times have I longed to surrender, to toss our power struggle away completely, to give myself over to Jude Jenkins and let him do whatever he wants to me? How many freaking times have I got myself off to that thought, my fingers moving busily under the covers?

Too many to count.

And it's like he peeled back my layers and shone a spotlight on my darkest, shadiest corners. My secret wishes and fears. My shame. Like Jude *sees* me, even in this, and I can't stand it. It's too much, too raw, too painful.

Jude Jenkins sees too much for his own good.

Because if we ever did *that*... if we acted out those secret daydreams, shedding our rivalry to become something more... that would require so much trust. Unconditional faith. And how could we ever have that after everything we've said and done? After all the traded insults; the constant sparring; the mean little pranks? The cutthroat competition and all the times we've said we hate each other?

The baggage between us two is overwhelming. It's a whole freaking mountain range of emotional suitcases piled high, one that would take every ounce of courage and strength to hike over. And even if we could get past all of that, even if we made it to the summit, there's the small matter of what I've *just* done, right here at this party.

The way I just rejected Jude so harshly, his dark blue eyes flared with pain and resentment. The way I did it in front of everyone too, like a complete jerk.

Tugging on my dress, I clear my throat.

So much regret. Music thumps across the rooftop, vibrating my bones, and my tongue is thick when I swallow.

Where did Jude go? Is he okay?

Does he *really* hate me now?

But it's no use: no matter how much I tug my dress straight, I can still feel my rival's hands on me, scorching my body through the silk. The ghost of his breath tickles my earlobe, and without his body heat pressed against my front, I shiver.

It's a cool night. The sun shone hot all day, baking this rooftop, but now the temperature has dropped and the cold breeze slices through my dress and chills my skin. The guys from the Legal department keep staring at me, laughing and whispering together, like we're all in high school rather than grown adults. Jeez.

My steps are wobbly as I weave back through the crowd, hunting for a pair of indigo eyes. Normally I'm good in heels, but after what just happened, I'm as trembly as a baby deer. There's a sick feeling in my stomach, this queasy certainty that I've gone badly wrong—that I've gone too far this time, and cracked this thing between us beyond repair.

Sure, Jude was kind of a dick. But I can't pretend to be shocked—can't act like we're just regular coworkers and he said something awful. The fact is we've been dancing around each other for *years,* stewing in sexual tension, and he didn't say anything that wasn't true. If I'm honest with myself, I *liked* it. I liked when he spoke to me like that, all husky and heated.

Oh, god.

What if he won't look at me on Monday?

Or what if he does, but he's all cold and distant?

Shit, what if Jude Jenkins won't tease me anymore? What if he treats me like everyone else, with polite professionalism?

I'm gonna throw up.

"There you are." Lucy appears at my side, worry pinching

her forehead. If she weren't my best friend I'd barely recognize her tonight, because gone is the cardigan and glasses and her neat auburn bun. Instead, my curvy bestie looks like a movie star. Her hair spills over her shoulder in glorious waves, and her red dress accentuates her hourglass figure. All around us, our coworkers do double-takes, squinting as they try to place Lucy as the mouse from the Accounts department. "Are you okay? You look pale."

"I'm fine." My throat is drier than the Sahara, but I'm not about to ruin Lucy's night too with my drama. Not when she dressed up like *this*, and somehow landed a date with the company heartthrob. Speaking of which… "Where's Darius?"

The blush that crawls up Lucy's chest can't be fake. Her smile is wobbly. "He's getting us drinks."

I force a smile. "That's sweet. Are you gonna tell me how you two wound up dating?"

To my surprise, Lucy's shoulders slump, and she won't meet my eye. "We're not… that is, tonight is more of, um…"

The band finishes one song and strikes up the next. Someone shrieks with laughter nearby, and the mist from the swimming pool snakes between our bare legs.

"A casual thing?" If I don't guess, we might never get there. Lucy's all folded over, fiddling with her bracelet, and I hate that my question burst her bubble so easily. How do I build her back up again?

"No." Darting a look at our nearby colleagues, Lucy leans in and whispers. "It's a practice run. To teach me how to date, you know? Darius heard me say I need practice and he, um. He offered to help."

He what?

"Darius Amin offered to fake date you." My voice is flat. "To

33

help you practice."

"Um. Yes."

"*The* Darius Amin."

AKA the guy all the receptionists swoon over. The man with the Hollywood good looks and model-worthy clothes. The man who makes incredible music and attracts big name stars to our agency. The Grapevine celebrity. That guy?

Sure, *I've* never been into him, because I've been wrapped up in my crush on Jude. But even I can objectively see: Darius Amin is a catch. And he's out here fake-dating people? Sneakily offering Lucy practice like it's no big deal?

Apparently Jude Jenkins is not the only agent of chaos in this company.

And maybe it's all fun and games to the composer, but the blush scorching my best friend's cheeks says it *means* something to her. She keeps biting her lip against a shy smile. My chest tightens, and god, I can't handle any more heartbreak tonight. It's been bad enough already.

So I mean well when I take Lucy's hand and squeeze her fingers. "You be careful, okay? Don't… don't put your heart on the line."

Her mouth curves down, but Lucy nods and squeezes my fingers back. "I won't. I've got this, Vi, I promise. I know a guy like Darius isn't really meant for a girl like me." And that's not what I meant at all, not the message I wanted to send, but Lucy glances over my shoulder and pastes a brave smile on her face. "He's coming now. Are you sure you're okay?"

Hm. Am I okay?

Well, judging by my knee-jerk public rejection of Jude and the way I just accidentally trampled my best friend's confidence, I'd say I'm a walking disaster. A wobbly, queasy disaster. Maybe

I should find a dark corner and stand there alone until I can trust myself not to hurt any more feelings. Maybe I should move to a tropical island and live as a hermit, surviving on crabs and coconuts. Yeah.

"I'm good." Lucy starts to turn away, but I tug her back gently by the hand. "You look beautiful, Luce. You're seriously such a bombshell, and any guy would be lucky to have you. Have fun tonight, okay?"

"Of course!" She hugs me, but I don't think my words sink in. Damn it. "You too. Knock Jude Jenkins dead."

Oof.

I'd rather wrap myself around his big, lean body and hug until he forgives my earlier outburst, but hey. That is less catchy.

Lucy turns and heads toward Darius, the crowd swallowing her whole. Everything in me aches as I watch her go.

Hugging my waist, I peer around the roof, searching for Jude, and failing that... a quiet spot to hide.

Jude

The trick to surviving parties like these is to find a home base. A secret spot with no other people around, preferably dark and quiet, where you can catch your breath and build up the willpower to get back out there again.

Tonight's home base: a shadowy strip of roof far away from the band and crowds, with a trellis to lean against. The city is lit up down there like a fallen galaxy.

Music and laughter drift over here too, but they're muted, carried off by a whistling breeze. And it's colder away from all that body heat, so cold that I shiver beneath my navy shirt. The whiskey I knock back scorches a trail down my throat.

I'd throw myself off this roof before kissing you, Jude Jenkins.

Those words play on a horrible loop in my brain. Round and round, until my gut aches and my temples throb.

Well, no one could accuse Violet Moore of mincing her words. She got her message across, that's for sure. I tip my glass back again, but it's empty, damn it, and only a few dregs trickle onto my tongue. Bending down, I place my glass on the floor with a sigh.

There's not enough whiskey in the world—but that brand of self destruction has never been my style. I prefer to torment the love of my life until she loathes my presence. That's my vice of choice.

My head is hazy as I straighten up, but not from the drink. I've got that dull, gnawing sense of horror—the kind which comes when you can't quite believe something is real. It's the same way I felt when I broke my ankle in college one week before our big basketball game; the same numbness that came over me as a ten year old kid hearing our family dog had died.

The numbness that says: *this can't be happening. This can't be real.*

Surely there's been some cosmic error; I can't truly have fallen madly in love with a woman who can't stand me. I'd like a refund please, universe.

"Shit." My head thumps back against the trellis, the leaves of a climbing vine rustling in response. This is not how I hoped tonight would go.

I pictured cool drinks, warm laughter, and trading friendly barbs with my beautiful rival. Violet rolling her eyes at me, her mouth twitching as she fights a smile; her soft voice in my ear on the dance floor, insulting me even as she presses closer. It seemed so clear, so inevitable, like a path laid in front of our feet.

Deluded. That's what I was.

Can't believe I called Hazel to check Violet would be coming tonight. Can't believe I thought there was something *real* between us; an undeniable connection. I need my head checked.

"Is this a pity party for one, or can anybody join?"

Violet's voice sends a pleased shudder down my spine. I stiffen where I'm leaning against the trellis, staring up at the stars.

Heels scrape against the stone roof. My rival approaches slowly, like I might spook at any sudden movements, and you know what? She's not wrong.

Need to get out of here. Whatever Violet wants from me right now, it's not something I can give, so I tug on my shirt collar and keep staring up at the night sky. My tone is light as I say, "It's a private party, I'm afraid. By invitation only."

She huffs a small laugh, and comes to stand by my side anyway.

Irritation snakes through my gut, coiling tight. What is she doing here? What does she *want*? Can't she see this is killing me?

"I'm hiding." Violet's confession is quiet, and her body heat seeps through my sleeve. "Tonight has been a disaster for me."

"Diddums," I say flatly.

And it's such a relief to hear her snort, to feel her shoulder nudge my arm, that suddenly I don't want her to leave after all. No: I want her here by my side, turning me inside out with how badly I want her. I want her private confessions and her teasing words, and I guess I have zero pride when it comes to this woman, because you know what? I don't care if she doesn't love me back.

I *need* her.

Tragic but true.

I'd rather spend the rest of tonight with Violet Moore, heartbroken and humiliated, than go back out to that party and be with anybody else.

How did I get here? How did she do this to me? Sometime

over the last few years, in between griping about my messy desk and trading insults by the water cooler, this woman got into my blood.

"You're a good dancer," Violet says.

"Thank you. You, on the other hand, are shit."

A sharp elbow digs into my ribs, but she's laughing. "I am not!"

Please. "You stepped on my foot at least five times, and in those heels too. I could sue you for millions."

"You won't, though."

"No." Sniffing hard, I frown up at the winking stars. They're faded by the city lights, the night sky made hazy by the constant glow, but I like to remember that even if we can't see it, there's a whole universe up there. Planets and black holes and asteroids. "Too much paperwork."

Violet hums, shuffling close so that our arms press together—and my heartbeat jolts in response, shuddering faster. What is she doing? What happened to being repulsed by me?

I fucking hate the hope blooming in my chest. When will I learn my lesson? When will I take a goddamn hint? Not tonight.

"I'll give you a do-over," I say, testing the waters. "If you want to defend your honor, this is your chance. One dance to prove you're not completely uncoordinated."

Violet's already turning to face me, and when I glance down, she looks hopeful in the gloom. The moonlight glints in her dark hair, and a cautious smile curves her lips.

Cautious? Violet Moore?

Body snatcher alert.

But when those slender arms loop around my neck, they're oh so familiar.

39

This. Yeah. This is how it feels to have Violet Moore against my chest: this is her berry scent and her soft warmth, and *that* is her foot stepping on mine. It's all perfect once again, and everything is right with the universe.

"Ouch."

"Sorry." Violet huffs, like I'm tricking her into stepping on my toes somehow. We turn in slow circles, too far away from the music to follow a beat. "Maybe if you didn't have such giant clown feet, I wouldn't step on them."

"Way to victim-blame. But hey, you know what they say." When I squeeze her waist, Violet's sudden blush scorches me like a space heater. Adorable. "Giant clown feet? That means a giant clown—"

"Don't!" Her face tucks in the crook of my throat, her shoulders shaking with laughter, and holy shit, I don't know what to do with myself. I'm grinning up at the stars like a loon. "Please, Jude. Do not say it. You'll give me nightmares."

That's fair. Clowns are awful.

Pressing my face against the top of her head, I breathe her in.

And maybe Violet doesn't want to date me. Maybe more than this is off limits. But perhaps if I'm patient, if I wait and hope and long from afar, Violet will learn to trust me.

Trust that when I tease her, it's with love.

When I challenge her at work, it's because I know she's the best.

And when we fight, it only makes me want her more. Makes me desperate to hold her.

"What a mess," Violet murmurs, and I grunt in agreement. Somehow, for two supposedly intelligent people, we have made a complete disaster out of this. "You know, I didn't mean what I said back there. I was embarrassed, and I lashed out. I'm sorry."

We turn in silence for a long moment.

I nudge her temple with my chin. "Please elaborate."

Another slow circle; another wince as she steps on my foot. Violet truly is an awful dancer, but somehow that just makes me love her more. Disastrous.

"You were right." She grits out the words, like it takes a huge effort. And I get it, because it takes every ounce of my willpower not to crow triumphantly and ruin the moment. "About what I wanted from you. *With* you. The stuff about... about kneeling, and um..."

"Begging?" My arms tighten in case she tries to escape, but Violet sighs and presses closer.

"Yes. You ass."

"I'm not bragging! Do you hear me bragging?"

"I don't hear you *not* bragging."

We lapse into silence, and I'm glad it's dark on this patch of rooftop. I can grin like an idiot, hidden in the gloom, and we can speak more honestly somehow in the shadows. It's easier to confess things in the dark.

"So." Violet's skin is soft when I cup her face. And we're not spinning anymore, not even pretending to dance, but I'm still dizzied by this moment. "If I kiss you, will you solemnly swear not to leap off this roof?"

Two hands fist in the front of my shirt and tug me closer. "Cross my heart," she says.

Well, then.

Our noses bump, and the trellis creaks in the breeze behind us. Violet's breath tickles my chin, and she's pushing up on her toes, even as I bend my neck to reach her. If this works out, I'll have to invest in a step ladder.

41

"Violet Moore." I grip the hair at the base of her neck, tilting her head back. Her lips part and she stares up at me, already glazed and breathing hard. "I've wanted this for so fucking long. You have no idea."

And thousands of heated daydreams about this moment have already flickered through my mind. We've had a lot of build up. So it seems impossible that when we finally kiss, it could ever live up to the hype, but our lips brush...

And my heart goes crazy.

Thump. Thump. Thump.

It slams against my ribs like a battering ram.

Thump. Thump. Thump.

Violet is scorching hot, melting against me, kissing me back, and I don't need air. Don't ever need to breathe again. Who needs oxygen, anyway? Not me. Don't need anything except Violet's hands tugging at my shirt and her body bowing against mine and the scrape of her teeth on my bottom lip. The faint sting of pain.

Figures that when we finally, *finally* break down and kiss, it's a battle for dominance. A power struggle, just like everything else in our fraught relationship. And that isn't what Violet confessed she wanted, it's not what she *really* needs from me, but maybe we're not there yet. Guess we can't go from zero to one hundred when it comes to trust.

That's fine.

I'll put the work in.

And in the meantime... this is the best fucking thing I've ever felt. Violet moans when I move to her throat, sucking and nibbling at her warm skin. Her breath hitches when I press a thigh between her legs, gripping her hips, encouraging her to rub against me. To ride my thigh right here in the dark.

"Oh my—*god*. Jude! Oh, shit. Holy shit."

Violet's babbling, lost in the moment. Incoherent. I love it so much. Love *her* so much, especially when she grabs my shoulders for balance and starts rocking, chasing the friction she needs. And maybe she's not kneeling or begging, but there's vulnerability in this too. There's a lot of trust brewing between us on this rooftop.

Plus it's really goddamn hot. The damp heat between her thighs sears through my pant leg, and Violet is such a goddess in the way she rolls her hips, head tipping back. In the way she gasps and grunts and bites her bottom lip, completely shameless in her pleasure as I kiss her throat, her earlobe, her cheek, her chin, any part of her I can reach. Her dress ripples in the moonlight.

One day I'll get Violet Moore naked and spread out on my mattress. One day soon I'll catalog every inch of her, kissing and tormenting until she loses her goddamn mind.

Yeah. *That's* the power struggle in our future. That's the way we'll one up each other from now on, competing to win.

I just need to show her that. Somehow.

Need to drag us to that promised land.

But for now as Violet stills, pleasure shuddering through her body, her eyes drift closed. She cuts me off; won't let me see. Won't give me anything except her fractured moan, and the way her limbs tremble as she comes and comes.

And as reality creeps back in, as Violet slowly returns back to herself, she retreats. An invisible shutter goes down behind her eyes, and the cold breeze slips beneath my collar, chilling my skin.

"Whoops." My rival stumbles back a step, tugging her dress straight, and she smiles at me, embarrassed. At least she's not yelling this time. "Guess I got carried away. Sorry about that."

Sorry? She's *sorry*? For the highlight of my life so far?

It's an effort to smile at her, sliding my hands into my pockets. If Violet needs to take a step back, if she needs things to be less intense for a minute, if she needs lighthearted Jude, I can give her that. Listen to me: I *will* be what she needs.

"Any time." I wink, and my chest burns when she rolls her eyes. "Consider me at your service, sweetheart."

I *will* break down those walls. Somehow or another, I'll do it. Nothing else matters.

Violet

~~~~

Sneaking back to join the party, it feels like there's a neon sign flashing above my head that says, "JUST HOOKED UP!" My hair is wind-ruffled, my cheeks are permanently hot, and I'm so swollen and slick between my legs, I feel like I'm walking funny.

Made Jude check the front and back of my dress for damp patches before we came back over here, shining his phone light on the silk. That was a new low.

But shockingly, he didn't mock me for that request. Didn't make me feel like a screw-up or even joke about the size of my ass. No: Jude Jenkins let me ride his thigh and then was a perfect gentleman in the aftermath, and it does not compute.

Who *is* he?

Who am I?

Gah. I need a drink.

"What would you like?" my rival asks now, nodding at the nearest pop up bar. It's twined with string lights, and a young guy in a white shirt and braces stands behind the bar, shaking

45

a cocktail to the band's beat. "Fair warning: if you say cyanide, you *will* hurt my feelings."

Pressing my lips together, I turn my face into the breeze. Sparks keep zipping under my skin, my nerves fizzing with excitement at what just happened between us. All around, our coworkers laugh and drink and joke and dance, like my whole world didn't just turn upside down at this party.

Did Jude like what we did?

Would he want to do it again?

"Violet?" He ducks down now, frowning at me with those indigo eyes. His dark hair is so thick and tuggable, and his lips are slightly red from our kiss. He looks debauched, and almost as wired as I feel. Like he poked an electrical socket and got shocked awake.

I love him.

Holy shit, I love this man.

This is terrible news!

"I'm getting you a water," Jude says, taking my elbow and steering me toward the bar. "You look like you might vomit, sweetheart, and I'm trying really hard not to be offended by that."

It's true. My insides are churning; my head is light. A clammy sweat has broken over my skin, and I can't feel my face. Since when am I in love?

A crush? Sure. Inconvenient sexual longings? Absolutely. But *love*?

"There, there." Jude rubs steady circles on my back, fussing over me with zero care for the stares we're attracting. It must be strange for these people too—they're all so used to watching us spat like alley cats. This truce must be confusing. "Would you like to go home? There's a car service, apparently."

46

"Yes." My spine straightens, and I'm still in a trance, but *that's it.* That's what I want right now. Need to get away from these stares and whispers and out of these stupid heels that are crushing my toes; need to go somewhere I can think straight. "Take me home. To *your* home."

Jude's eyes flare with heat, and he draws in a long inhale. When he nods, his jaw is tight.

"I won't expect anything." He pulls out his phone, tapping at the screen.

"Always such low expectations of me."

"No, I—"

When he glances up, I wink.

And as that smile bursts over his face, crinkling his eyes… my heart trembles like a leaf. Oh, boy.

* * *

Turns out Jude Jenkins does not live on a trash heap out at the city limits. My bad. Instead, he lives in a small but tasteful one-bedroom apartment not far from work, with a leafy park view, bare brick walls, and metal beams on the ceiling.

There's barely any mess. Only a normal amount of clutter. I feel misled.

"Welcome to Casa Jenkins," Jude says, strolling across his living room floor. It's all open plan, airy and calm, and there's an abstract painting of aspen trees on one wall. "Can I get you that water? Or would you like something stronger?"

Sinking down onto the arm of the sofa, I kick off my heels and stretch out my aching feet. "You know, if you wanted to date me, you shouldn't have pretended to be a hopeless hoarder."

"Didn't put you off, though, did it?" Jude twinkles with

amusement, then crosses to his refrigerator to rummage inside. Jars clink together, and his voice bounces around the small space as he calls, "Not my fault if you have low standards, Moore."

It's different, scoffing at him now.

Warmer. Fond.

Or—maybe it was *always* fond, but I was kidding myself. Pretending we were enemies when all along, we were building... this.

My toes scrunch against his black and white rug. The big windows are dark, with the city lights glittering out there, and our faint reflections shift in the glass.

I look small. Nervous, perched on the sofa arm.

My dress looks awesome though, rippling down my body like a waterfall. Thrift stores forever!

"You look ready to flee," Jude observes, walking over to press a bottle of ginger ale into my hand. "There. That should help with your stomach."

"Thanks." The sip fizzes against my tongue, both fiery and sweet, but the truth is, I don't feel queasy anymore. Every minute I spend with Jude in this new reality, this world where we make out and tease each other and nothing blows up, I feel more and more settled.

This is... right.

This is how things are meant to be.

Me and him. Jude and I. In each other's apartments, sipping drinks, chatting idly; leaving parties together and sharing a ride home.

What took us so long? Am I really that blind? That stubborn?

"So does this truce mean that you'll finally clean your desk?" My heart pitter-patters as Jude draws closer. He swigs from

48

his own ginger ale, the pale column of his throat shifting as he swallows, and I can't tear my eyes away from him. Can't even blink.

He's so freaking *handsome*. Tall and dark-haired and lean and broad-shouldered, with those inky blue eyes and that devilish smile. It's a miracle that I resisted him for so long—a feat of extreme human endurance.

"Maybe." He sets his bottle on the coffee table, then slides his hands into his pockets, watching me steadily. "Maybe I'll find new ways to torture you."

A shiver ripples down my spine.

And he sees it.

He sees *everything*.

But Jude smiles, slow and teasing. I lean over and place my own bottle down with a soft thump, nerves squirming in my belly.

This is it. I—I don't know what *it* is, exactly, but we've definitely been building to something, and after how kind and thoughtful Jude was earlier... maybe I'm finally ready to do this. To trust him.

Maybe I can be brave too.

"Do you want to stop fighting all the time, Violet?" He watches me steadily.

I lift one shoulder, chewing on my bottom lip. The truth is, I'm not sure about that. I *like* fighting with Jude. It shocks me awake; makes me feel alive. Bantering back and forth with Jude Jenkins feels like bungee jumping. It's a non-stop thrill.

But do I want it to get in the way of *this*? Of us?

Nope, I do not.

My feet jiggle on the rug. "Depends on the context, I suppose."

Jude grins. "Atta girl."

And... what he said earlier was true. Maybe I like bickering at work, maybe I like tormenting each other during normal conversations, but there's a deep, secret part of me that wants to surrender to this man sometimes. To stop fighting, stop *resisting*, stop constantly trying to prove something.

What would that be like? How would it feel?

My heart skitters at the thought.

"We can keep tussling if you like." Jude tilts his head. "Or you can let me be in charge for once."

The apartment is silent except for the muffled sounds of traffic outside. It's comfortably warm in here, but goosebumps raise on my bare arms.

I wet my lips. "Okay."

Jude's eyebrows bounce up. "Okay? Really?"

"Yes." Blowing out a harsh breath, I nod. "Okay."

One tiny word, one giant leap of faith. But I can do this. I *can*. And a whole slideshow of emotions flicker across Jude's face—triumph, joy, relief, nerves—but he schools his features and crooks a finger at me.

"Alright. Come here, sweetheart."

I stand, heart in my throat. The rug is soft beneath my feet. And my habits are screaming at me to lash out, to slide back into our automatic battle, but a deeper instinct overrides them all.

My steps are quiet. Jude's chest rises and falls as I reach him, the top two buttons of his navy shirt opened to bare his throat.

His breaths are shaky, too. That makes me feel a little better, because we're both off-kilter. Both reeling from this, but pushing forward anyway.

"You are so fucking gorgeous." Jude runs a fingertip up my

wrist, my arm, all the way to my shoulder where he draws a little circle. "Like someone took all my favorite things, all my secret desires, and built you for me in a lab."

My voice scrapes. "Narcissistic much?"

Jude chuckles and leans down, his breath tickling my throat. And... *heat.*

That's what I feel when he kisses me there. The gentle press of his mouth, the flick of his tongue, sends a molten wave of heat surging through my veins. Jude's barely done anything yet, only kissed beneath my jaw, and already my nipples are two hard beads and I'm arching toward him, whimpering. Needy.

It's so shameless. So *vulnerable.* And doubt spears through me, frazzling my brain, but Jude chases that doubt away as fast as it came, kissing along my jaw before claiming my mouth.

His arms wrap around me, sealing me to his chest.

His hold is strong, sure, possessive.

After all those fears, after staying tensed up for so long, it's the easiest thing in the world to melt into his strength. To let him tilt my head back and kiss me hard, tongue sliding into my mouth; to switch my brain off for once in my goddamn life and surrender to the present moment.

I love this man.

I want him badly.

And I'm done hiding that. Done fighting the facts.

"So," Jude says between kisses, "fucking—gorgeous."

Golden warmth suffuses my limbs. And this is the world's best spa treatment, the most relaxed I've ever been, so when Jude finally nudges me to kneel, I float down there on a happy little cloud.

Thump. The rug tickles my knees. I don't mind, though—I could be kneeling on hot coals right now and I'd struggle to

51

care. Not when Jude places my hands on his hips and leaves them there, working his belt open with a creak of black leather.

Yes. Finally.

This is what I want. This is what I've dreamed of.

Kneeling for him. Pleasing him.

But Jude flicks his top button open then pauses. "Are you sure about this?" Worry creeps into his low voice. "Because if you change your mind, we can stop at any time—"

"Duh." My smile is dreamy; his shirt is soft beneath my fingertips. I scratch at his waist, marveling at the hard muscles hidden below the fabric. "I know that. Keep going."

There's a steadying huff, then the scratch of his zipper is loud in the quiet room. My heartbeat booms in my ears, and this close I can smell his laundry powder. Can feel his body heat against my front.

Jude draws out his cock and strokes it once. My eyes practically cross as I try to get a good look at it, because it's long and thick and weirdly handsome, and I guess I wasn't the only one built in a lab. Jude Jenkins is perfect all over, and he smells freaking amazing. Like soap and the faint scent of musk.

"Look at you." His mouth curves up, and he strokes himself again. "Look at you squirming down there, Violet. You're needy, aren't you, sweet girl? You want a taste."

My head nods quickly, with zero input for my brain, and my mouth opens. My tongue pokes out, and this is so *much*, oh god, I'm a puppet on his strings, so embarrassing, but Jude doesn't mock me for a second. A hiss escapes between his teeth, and his face is stark with hunger as he aims his shaft for my mouth.

As soon as the head rubs over my tongue, I close my lips around him with a moan. Tastes so *good*. Salty and perfect.

So right.

My head bobs for him, my spit slicking up his shaft. Those pained little grunts of pleasure Jude's making—this is how things should be.

At last.

"Fuck," he says, hands fisting in my hair. He's not gentle, and that's perfect too, because the slight twinge of pain keeps me rooted, keeps this real. "Oh, *fuck*, Violet. That mouth. That hot little mouth."

He's thrusting steadily, frowning down with pure focus. Our ragged breaths fill the air. My cheeks hollow as I suck, and I've never been so wet and achy in my life. I'm so swollen between my legs, I can't bear to sit back on my heels.

So. Good.

And I'd happily do this for hours, would happily suck and suck all night long, floating in this dream state, but Jude curses abruptly and pulls out with a pop, a string of spit glistening between his cock and my lower lip. I sway on my knees, gasping for breath.

"Alright." Jude joins me on the rug, two angry slashes of red on his cheekbones, and he crowds me back until I tip onto my ass, giggling. "You're going to do this, sweetheart. You're going to beg for me. Come on, you can do it."

And I know I was embarrassed before, so ashamed for wanting this; I know I thought I'd never be able to go through with it. Could never beg my rival for his cock.

But I didn't account for the terrible ache between my legs.

Didn't account for the giddy, floaty feeling that sucking him would give me.

Didn't account for how warm and happy and *free* I'd feel at the mercy of Jude Jenkins, and the fierce pride he'd show in me at every step of the way. This is heaven.

So it's easy to let him crowd me back, propping my weight on my hands behind me. It's easy to gaze up at my arch enemy, and hook my legs around his hips, and urge him toward me with my heels, my silken dress pooling around us in a silvery puddle.

"Please," I say, smiling as a shudder rolls through Jude's whole body. He loves this too, you know. We're perfectly matched in every way. "*Please*, Jude. Please fuck me. I need it. I need it so, so badly."

Jude

Hearing Violet Moore beg for my cock is the sweetest thing I've ever heard. How have I survived without it for so long? All I know is the world has been in dull gray-scale, and now it's bursting into bright technicolor. Angels blow tiny trumpets high up in the clouds.

Of course I'm going to give it to her.

Of course I'm going to make her feel good.

Nothing else matters in the whole goddamn universe except making Violet's toes curl, and making her voice hoarse from screaming my name. Obviously.

When I prowl forward, flipping her dress up and lining our bodies together, she's already soaking wet. Already whimpering, her hips rocking up to meet mine.

I slide her cream lace thong to one side, thumb skimming over the trimmed dark strip of hair on her mound. And Violet quivers, her thick thighs dropping wider for me, her head tilting back with a sigh. She's so responsive, wound so tight that a single brush of my fingertip is enough to make her whole body clench and roll.

"You're mine," I tell her, rubbing my bare shaft along her seam. I'm already slicked up with her spit, already shiny and wet and so hard it hurts, but there's no way I'm rushing this. No way I'll rush *her*. "Violet? You're mine."

"I—I know." She's nodding along, her bottom lip bitten red. Pearly white teeth sink into that plump lip, and I trace her mouth with my thumb, then nudge past her lips until she sucks me to the second knuckle, her eyes glazed with pleasure.

Her tongue swirls around me, and her cheeks hollow.

Christ.

Gritting my teeth, I count backward from ten. Are you listening, universe? I will not, I repeat, will *not* finally get Violet Moore to beg for this, then embarrass myself in two minutes flat. Not happening.

But I'm overheating under my clothes, and my muscles are tense on my bones. My heart's thumping hard enough to bruise, and there's a knife of pleasure stabbing in my gut.

Back and forth, I rock.

Up and down her slit, parting her with my shaft.

"Please," Violet whispers again, the word muffled around my thumb. "Please, Jude. I need it. Need *you*."

God damn.

"Alright." Hitching one of her thighs higher, I line up with her entrance. "Alright, sweetheart. I'm here."

And every ounce of my awareness narrows in on the tip of my cock as it presses inside her body. Her tight, hot, *slick* channel sucks me deeper as her inner muscles quiver, and she's so good, so good, so good.

Violet is really fucking tight. *Really* tight. I pause, pulse hammering.

"Are you—?"

"Uh-huh." She nods, gifting me another dreamy smile. I lean back, stunned.

And in another life, this is the part where Violet would warn me not to mock her; where she'd search for some vulnerability in me too, to make it even. Where she'd stiffen up and lash out, and everything would fracture apart.

But tonight Violet rolls her hips up to me, and sighs when I bend down to kiss her neck. She's not embarrassed that this is her first time. Not clenching up with distrust.

Because she's *mine*.

Holy shit. Finally.

"This is the only cock you've ever begged for, huh?" If my body temperature climbs another degree, I'll burst into flame. She's mine. All mine. "Well, it's the only one you'll ever need. I'm gonna make you feel so fucking good, Violet, you'll never even wonder about another man."

She snorts, winding one arm around my neck, and nuzzles me back. "Jude? You're worried about nothing. I'm already there."

And there's no way I'm this lucky, no way I'll ever deserve such a prize, but I swear, I'll spend my whole life working to make this woman happy. Pressing forward, I grit my teeth against the hot squeeze of her body.

She's tense at first.

Braced for pain.

But as I coax her to relax, as I kiss and stroke and tease, Violet melts back against the rug and I cover her completely.

One long, deep thrust.

Another.

Another.

Her body adapts to me quickly, getting slicker, giving way, until we're sealed together as tight as we can go, rocking together on the rug.

"I love you," I mutter into her hair. "Have I told you that yet?"

Her laugh is bright, echoing around my apartment.

Pushing up onto my hands, I start to give it to her harder. Her curves jiggle beneath that silk, and Violet's head tilts from side to side as she moans and whimpers.

Pink cheeks, mussed up bangs, and the slick sounds of our bodies joining. Need to remember this. Need to commit every last detail to memory.

She's mine.

All mine.

And Violet sighs so sweetly when I reach between our bodies, rubbing her clit. She tilts her head to let me lick and nibble her neck, then squeezes my waist with those magnificent thighs, urging me on.

We're not fighting.

Not grappling for dominance.

For once in our lives, we're working together. Chasing a shared goal: that spot inside Violet that makes her breath hitch and her blush deepen, the spot which makes her clamp down on me like a vise. And every time I hit it, I chase her higher toward her peak, until she's spread out beneath me, trembling.

"Oh—oh god. *Jude.* Oh god."

Sweat trickles down my spine beneath my shirt. Gonna bundle us both into the shower after this. Gonna clean us off and then lick between Violet's legs until she slumps against the tiles. But first—

"You're so goddamn perfect. Come for me. Let go, sweetheart. Trust me."

She bites down hard on her lower lip, head thrashing, stomach muscles clenching.

My lungs freeze.

And I *feel* it. Every twitch and gasp and ripple of pleasure. Every blissful shudder that rocks her frame. I feel Violet Moore come apart from the inside, feel the evidence of her trust in me, and it makes me brand new.

When I follow her over the edge a minute later, grunting and pumping her full… it's a sticky slice of heaven.

* * *

Two years later

It's quiet in the office today. Phones bleat and keyboards tap and the water cooler glugs, but it's calm for a Friday morning. Sighing, I open my email and scan through the newest contracts.

This job is fine.

Fun, even. I get to work on cool projects, get to be creative with big budgets, and boss around an army of minions—I mean, interns. But it's not the same when Violet's gone.

Leaning back in my chair, I scowl at the elevator doors, arms folded over my chest. Any minute now.

The sign above the elevator lights up, counting through the floors. I swallow hard, chest rioting.

Even now, after two years together, Violet makes my heart go crazy. What's the manly version of butterflies? Bats? She gives me bats in my stomach.

The elevator pings, and the doors slide open.

Violet strolls out into the office, a tote bag slung on her

shoulder and one hand resting on her baby bump beneath her shirt dress.

"Judas." My wife pokes her tongue out at me, settling into the chair opposite mine. Not long now until her maternity leave begins—and not long until I strike out and start my own agency, becoming my own boss. I've dawdled and dragged my feet for a couple years, too eager to see Violet at work every day, but our growing baby has given me that extra push. Time to up my game. To *provide*.

Violet can always come work for me, too. If she wants.

Sparks will surely fly.

"Falafel again?" I nod at her tote bag as she places it on the desk, some mystery wrapper rustling inside. "You're a sucker for those coupons."

"Aaaand there goes your free bite." Violet grins, shifting in her chair until it squeaks. "Now who's the sucker? Hope you enjoy your crappy little ham sandwich for lunch."

Excuse me? "I made that!"

Violet grins wider. "Exactly."

And I hope we never stop sparring. Hope these sparks never, ever die out.

My wife is the best enemy I ever had.

II

Faking It with Her Crush

Description

He's the company heartthrob. **The man all the interns swoon over.**

And he's teaching me how to flirt.

Darius and I are good friends. It's easy to chat to a man I have zero chance with, because let's face it: *I'm* not the kinda girl he wants.

I'm bookish and curvy. Serious and shy, while he breaks hearts with a single smile.

But I'm tired of going to bed lonely every night, so when Darius offers me a fake date for practice, I think: what's the harm?

I'll remember it's all pretend. I won't get carried away by the moment.

And I *definitely* won't put my heart on the line…

Lucy

ne year ago

The first time I meet Darius Amin, I'm huddled in an office supply closet. Shelves of pens, staplers, notepads and envelopes loom on every wall, and I'm gripping a pack of highlighters and counting down from one hundred.

Sometimes I get overwhelmed, you know? Sometimes the world out there, even in the Accounts department, gets to be too much, and I need a minute. So this supply closet is my escape hatch; my chosen place to run and hide.

Not for long.

Just long enough to breathe, and count, and pick out pretty highlighters, clutching the pack with clammy hands. Any second now, I'll go back out there and pretend I was never gone, keeping my head down like a good worker.

The ring of phones drifts through the closed door, and it's dusty in here. Makes my nose itch. The whole space is lit by a single light bulb, dangling on a string overhead. It's not the nicest space, but when the panic comes on without warning, rising and crashing like the tide, I'll take whatever I can get.

Privacy.

A small, enclosed space—like a safe little burrow.

And pretty new highlighters for my planner.

Okay: in… out. In… out. Wrinkling my nose at the dust, I breathe slowly, still counting down through the sixties.

Voices drift past the closet, their footsteps coming so close the door rattles, and I stiffen against the nearest shelf. But the voices fade, and I gust out a long sigh, rubbing my thumb along the plastic packet edge.

Why?

Why do I get like this?

Why are the smallest things in life so freaking *hard* for me sometimes? Because ninety percent of the time, I am Capable Lucy. Reliable Lucy. The girl people bring their myriad problems to, with blind faith that I will come up with a solution. Then, once in a while, it's like a switch gets flipped in my brain, and I wind up… here.

Breathing dust.

Sweating into my cardigan.

Hoping and praying that no one catches me in this state. What would they say? What would they *think*? Anxious tears brim in my eyes, and I blink them away, tugging my pencil skirt straight. No time for that level of meltdown. Not here. I've got spreadsheets to work on.

So when Darius Amin opens the door without warning, slipping inside the supply closet, I'm on the tail end of my meltdown. My breaths are more even, my cheeks are cooling, and my eyes are dry. I've patted down my hair and given myself a little pep talk, ready to get back out there and face the world.

Lucy

Then *he* slides into my space: the man I've only ever seen from a distance in this company. The star composer who creates the music for all our videos; the heartthrob who makes all the interns swoon. With his dark, wavy hair flopping over his forehead, soulful brown eyes and bronze skin, Darius Amin is even more startling close-up.

He must move like a panther to sneak in here like that without warning. The walls on this floor are so thin, the doors vibrate in their frames whenever someone sits down too hard.

"Oh." Darius blinks at me, jerking to a stop. "Hello."

Crowded back against the shelves, I give an awkward wave. "Hi."

And it's mortifying to be caught like this, *suffocating* to be with a man like this in a space so small, but Darius's broad shoulders block the exit, and he's too busy staring at me to move.

Staring.

Frowning slightly, thick eyebrows pinched.

Probing me from head to toe, his warm brown gaze roaming over my cardigan, my tights, my simple flats, and back up to my blushing face.

"Are you alright?" Darius asks, ducking down to meet my eye.

His voice is deep and smooth, like rich melted chocolate. It raises the tiny hairs on my arms, and I wrap myself in a hug like I can save myself from this indignity.

From losing my head over the company heartthrob.

Swooning like all those interns.

I may not be a heart-stopper myself, but a girl needs *some* pride, damn it, and Darius Amin is not the kind of man for me.

I knew it from a distance, and it's been confirmed a hundred-fold up close, because it turns out Darius really is tall and graceful with movie-star good looks, while I'm a bookish, curvy accountant with tortoiseshell glasses.

We are not on the same level. And yet he's still looking at me like *that*, with equal parts concern and curiosity. What is going on?

"I'm fine." The words scrape out of my throat, but I raise my chin, daring my interloper to deny it. "I came in here for highlighters." Up waves Exhibit A. "Better get back out there."

And I've said all the right things, made all the right moves to leave, but Darius Amin still stands in front of the door, peering at me. My tummy squirms. "It's Lucy, isn't it?"

Um. Yeah.

But how does he know my name? This is a pretty big office, and our paths have never crossed before. Did he see me and ask someone who I was? Did he notice me the way I noticed him?

No. That's ridiculous.

That's a love-struck intern level of delusion.

"Yes. And you're Darius?"

Cringe. As if everyone in this building doesn't know the composer's name.

But he smiles, slow and warm. "That's me. Nice to finally meet you, Lucy."

Finally? Finally meet me? What does *that* mean? And why is he opening the door for me like that, waving me out into the corridor like a gentleman?

"We should get coffee," Darius says, his words ringing in my shocked ears. He turns and leans in the supply closet doorway, still pinning me with that intense gaze. "Something tells me we would be great friends."

68

Friends.

…Right.

My stomach sinks, but I force myself to nod and smile, fiddling with the highlighter packet. "That would be lovely."

Because of course he only wants to be friends. What else would Darius Amin want from me? And I should be happy, not queasy and disappointed, because friends are a blessing.

Even startlingly handsome friends.

"Tomorrow?" Darius presses. He really wants this coffee, huh?

My head nods, mechanical.

Guess I just befriended the company heartthrob. Huh.

My stomach churns all the way back to my desk.

Lucy

ᕙᕗᕙᕗ

P resent day

If one more person bursts into my cubicle begging me to fix their monthly report, I will throw a stapler at their head. Yes, I like to help my coworkers out when I can, but I'm only one person! There are a dozen accountants on this floor! Did someone write the word 'schmuck' on my forehead while I was sleeping last night?

Huffing and puffing and muttering under my breath, I rattle through another set of corrections, my fingers thundering over the keyboard. Finished my own report yesterday, of course.

All around, people bustle around the office, chatting and laughing by the water cooler, or arguing on the phone. The air smells like carpet cleaner, warm paper from the printer, and strong coffee. It's a bright day, and sunshine spears through the half-lowered blinds to cook us at our desks.

My chair squeaks as I spin around, snatching up my calculator and double-checking the numbers.

I *love* numbers.

Numbers are concrete. Absolute. They tell a clear story, and if you can read them, you can make sense of the world.

This world, anyway. The world of accounts and spreadsheets and frazzled clients calling us on the phone, asking us to explain every single charge on their invoices. Numbers are armor.

I don't even notice Darius until he clears his throat behind me. I whirl around, heart slamming, to find him leaning against my cubicle wall, stroking the stem a potted plant with a long, elegant finger.

The leaves shiver.

I do, too.

But my shoulders square, and I tamp down all those knee-jerk reactions I always have around this man: the fluttering pulse, the squirmy stomach, the heat climbing my throat. No time for that nonsense. I wrestle my body into submission and smile at my friend.

"Luce," Darius drawls, brown gaze flicking to mine. "I think you need more plants."

Ha. As if. With just one more pot squeezed into the explosion of greenery I'm building up in my cubicle, I could charge tourists for entrance.

"They're relaxing." My heart thuds beneath my blouse. "Plants lower our cortisol. It's scientifically proven."

Darius smiles as I yank off my glasses and polish them on my cardigan, wiping away this morning's stress-smudges. "Clearly. Is everyone working you into the ground up here?"

"Yup."

And the composer is a regular visitor in my cubicle—regular enough that I keep an extra chair for him, half-submerged in leaves—so I return to my work, fingers flying over the keyboard. He won't be offended. Plants rustle as Darius slides past, sinking into his chair behind me, and damn it, I can't focus with him back there.

His gaze is hot against the back of my neck.

The cedar scent of him makes me breathe faster, gulping down air.

And... I can't think straight. The numbers all blur together.

So I throw up my hands and give up, turning to face Darius where he's lounging, one ankle crossed over his knee.

"Don't mind me." His handsome face breaks into a smile, and oh, he's *so* good looking. It's not fair to us mere mortals. Because some of us need to focus, damn it, and not make asses of ourselves in front of men who see us only as friends.

Friends.

It hurts being this close to a man who I dream about every night, and who is oblivious to me... but I can't give Darius up. Even as only a friend, I'm addicted to him.

To his gentle humor and patience.

To his teasing glances and the coffee he brings me first thing every morning, always with some kind of warm pastry in a paper bag.

Not to mention his beauty and intelligence and the way he makes me feel more *grown up*, somehow, like someone who should be taken seriously.

Yeah. I can't quit Darius Amin. Not even when every rumor about him dating this receptionist or that intern makes my poor, bruised heart shrivel and ache. Not even when every flushed, sticky daydream I have about him makes me feel horribly guilty.

I mean, it's not like I can help it. Believe me, if I could kill this crush, I'd snipe it in a heartbeat. I'd snap its neck, hit man style.

"Can I help you with something? Why are you hiding in my cubicle this time?" Tapping my chin, I pretend to think. "Let me guess. You winked and caused a stampede among the admin assistants, and now you're hiding from all your admirers up here."

Darius's eyes twinkle, and he relaxes back in the chair. "You seriously overestimate my effect on women, Luce. Why is that, I wonder?"

Ugh. Where's that stapler? I've found a new target.

"Don't kid yourself, Amin. Some of us are immune to your charms," I lie.

"So you say."

See... *this* is why I can never squish the final embers of my crush for Darius. I give myself all these stern lectures about how he's not interested in me, about how it's been a whole year and he's never made a move, but then Darius will flirt, he'll say something like *that,* and I'm back to square one. Back to wondering.

Hoping.

Longing.

It would be cruel except Darius really doesn't know how I feel. He has no idea that these tiny moments of flirtation with him hurt me more than a whole failed relationship would with someone else.

I mean, probably. As an eternally single girl, I wouldn't really know. Too busy mooning after this roguish composer.

"So," Darius says. "Hot date for the party tonight?"

I scoff, fogging my own glasses. "Hardly."

It's our office's anniversary party. Ten years of Grapevine Creative Agency, celebrated on a skyscraper rooftop with a live band and an open bar. It's all anyone's talked about for months, and of course I'm going, but Darius's question sticks me with a sliver of doubt.

Is *he* bringing a date? Will I have to watch that? Will I have to laugh and chat and make polite conversation with whichever lucky woman won him for the night, all as punishment for crushing on my friend?

Maybe I'll fake a headache. Rooftop parties are probably super windy anyway, and yes, I bought that amazing dress—but I'm not sure I can pull it off.

"No one's caught your eye, huh?" Darius rubs his firm jaw, considering. "That's fair. I can't believe anyone would ever deserve you, Luce."

And that is *so* far from the problem that I can't help my bitter laugh. "As if. No, someone would have to ask me first, Darius. I have zero practice at dating. I'm twenty five years old and I've never even been kissed."

The composer's eyes flare with surprise, and I replay my words with mounting horror.

Never. Been. Kissed.

Why? Why did I tell him that? Aah! Why did I just confess to my all-consuming crush that I'm a twenty five year old virgin, and no one wants me? The sounds of the busy office swell and blur together, mingling with my rattling pulse, and Darius's lips move, but I don't hear the words.

"Huh?"

"I said I'll help you. I'll be your practice, if you want." Darius smiles at me, sunny and calm, like he just offered me a cupful of sugar rather than *dating practice*. What the—? "We could go to the party together. I'll show you off; build up your confidence. Let you feel what a real date is like."

A date with Darius Amin would be unlike a date with any other man. This, I am sure of, just like I'm sure this idea is a one-way street to a broken heart. How can I pretend to date the man I'm already madly in love with? How would I survive that? But…

"O-okay," my treacherous mouth says. "Sure."

Gah!

Darius blinks and straightens in his chair, like he didn't expect me to agree. "Ah… good. Good! So I'll pick you up at seven?"

Throat too tight to speak, I nod.

Darius leaves in a rustle of foliage, and I'm left with clammy hands and a fizzy, swooping feeling in my chest.

A fake date with my handsome friend.

With the charmer who breaks hearts everywhere he goes.

What am I thinking?

Darius

What the hell am I thinking?

Visiting Lucy in her cubicle is one thing. Befriending her and bringing her coffees and soaking up her presence like a sponge absorbing water—that's all fine. None of that crosses the invisible line I've drawn in my head.

But a *date*?

A fake practice date to build up her confidence for other men? A dress rehearsal before she heads out into the world for the real thing? Have I lost my goddamn mind?

My agitated strides carry me across the office, through the corridor and out into the stairwell. This building has an elevator, so there's no need to pound my way down flight after flight of stairs, except adrenaline has flooded my system and if I don't burn it off, I might punch a wall.

And that's not me. Darius Amin never gets worked up. Darius Amin never makes a scene. I'm always cool, supremely collected, channeling whatever inner turmoil I have into music.

Then Lucy comes along, and everything is jumbled. Fuck.

My shoes smack against the steps, echoing in the empty stairwell, and I'm breathing hard. The sound is ragged. If anyone catches sight of me now, they'll think I've lost my mind, and you know what? They'll be right.

A date.

A *date.*

A practice date with Lucy, the woman I want but can never have. The woman I will never be good enough for, who I should have stayed away from a year ago. But Lucy kept drawing me in from a distance, taunting me with those cute little glasses and prim outfits until I snapped. Now look at us.

Lucy thinks I have a constant revolving door of dates, and has never seen past my looks. Not enough to realize that those rumors are all bullshit.

Meanwhile I'm hopelessly gone for her.

Christ.

"You've really done it this time." My mutter bounces around the stairwell, and I keep pounding down, down, down all the flights of stairs, trying and failing to outrun the emotions squeezing my chest. When I finally burst out of the fire exit into an alley, I'm sweating under my dark green shirt, breathing hard through my nose.

Pigeons scatter, fluffing up their feathers and cooing. This is a quiet space, with swept cement and cigarette burns scorched into the wall. The sun doesn't reach here, and it smells like damp stone, moss and bird mess.

It's no paradise, but I linger anyway. Cursing myself and kneading my forehead, even as I *know* I won't take my offer back.

A night with Lucy?

A *date*—even a practice one?

This is a once in a lifetime experience.

* * *

"Remind me again why I've decided to die alone."

Thirty minutes later I'm on the top floor, my breathing calm and my clothes smoothed, strolling around the boss's office and squinting at the artwork on his walls. Leo Corbin favors abstract paintings—explosions of colors and emotion without obvious form. I'm more of an art deco man, myself.

The sun-drenched city stretches away through the huge glass windows. The cars and buses down there look like toys.

Leo blows out a long-suffering breath, flicking through a contract on his desk and ignoring me completely. He's been like this since our college days: prickly and ice-cold. From the outside, I seem warmer—certainly more socially adept— but deep down, I share Leo's same exhaustion and withdrawal from life. That's why when he asked me to join Grapevine as a composer, I agreed in seconds—he's my brother in everything except blood.

"You know, the longer you ignore me, the longer I'll bother you."

It's best to be clear with Leo. Straightforward. I learned that when we roomed together in freshman year, and nearly came to blows most weeks in the first semester. Christ, we hated each other's guts.

But by the spring, we'd figured it out. Found each other's wavelengths. And though neither of us would admit it out loud, we've been committed to this friendship ever since. It's bedrock.

"You're very needy for a famous composer." Leo turns a contract page, scowling down at the small print—and he has the same thick dark hair as me, but he's paler, with a square jaw and icy blue eyes. The boss would have interns slipping him love notes too if he didn't give off such clear Do Not Disturb vibes.

Maybe I should take a leaf out of Leo's book. Be less approachable—because I don't *want* those damn love notes, and they're causing me nothing but trouble. They're why Lucy will never, ever see me as a romantic possibility.

"Leo." Tucking my hands into my pockets, I stare blandly at the boss. He's barricaded behind his desk, hiding from the world in his work. Same as always. Outside his office, the soft, sweet voice of his assistant Hazel seeps under the door, but her words are muffled. "I'm having a meltdown here. Schedule me in."

With an almighty huff, Leo looks up—and frowns harder. He drops his pen.

"Christ. You look like shit."

Thank you.

"I feel like shit." Spreading my arms, I step closer to the huge desk. "So, go on. Make it all better."

Leo scoffs, but he's leaning back in his chair now, stroking his jaw. Hitting me with his full, monstrous focus. "I'm neither your daddy or your shrink. What do you want me to say?"

I already told him. "Remind me why I've decided to die alone."

It's a morbid pledge we made as college students, half-joking at the time. Poking fun at ourselves, even as we despaired at any alternatives. And yet we're in our thirties now, and neither of us shows any sign of breaking that oath, so I guess it was

79

more serious than we let on.

Leo rolls his neck, his gaze flitting to the closed door. Hazel laughs out there, her voice trilling in the quiet. "You know why."

Yeah. I do.

Because Leo and I both came from shitty, broken families with parents that hated each other *and* us. Because we've seen firsthand how impossible love is, how it's all such a fairy tale, and we each vowed not to put ourselves through that pain again. Not to bring any more kids into it, either.

But that was then. Before Lucy. Before spending another decade in the world, and seeing it's not all black and white. There are shades of gray; there's room for nuance. Almost nothing is all good or all bad, except for that prim little accountant, who came straight down from heaven.

"Things change," I say.

Leo grunts his disagreement. For the big boss up here in his steel and glass tower, nothing changes unless he gives his say-so.

But I try again. "There's this girl in Accounts—"

"Then fuck her," Leo cuts in. "Take her out a few times, and get her out of your system." The sweet assistant's muffled voice has gone silent outside the door. It's quiet enough to hear every rustle of clothing and the wind moaning outside the windows, up here halfway to the clouds. "But don't kid yourself, Darius. You and me... we're not meant for that shit. Remember? That's for people who grew up with the white picket fence and half a clue about love. That's for people who were wired right. Not us."

Yeah. Okay.

I nod, a sickly feeling churning in my gut. Because Leo's

never wrong, and he's not wrong about this either—if I ever got a chance with Lucy, I'd wreck it. Wreck *her*.

And I couldn't bear that. Couldn't live with myself if I hurt that sweet girl, but I've never seen a healthy relationship up close. Never had that modeled for me. I don't have the first clue.

"You're right." My chest burns, but I straighten my wristwatch. "I'll keep my distance."

Lucy

❧ ∞ ❧

There are ten minutes left until Darius picks me up for our date, and I just stabbed myself in the eye with a mascara wand. Now one eye is bloodshot and watering, the lashes all clumped, and mascara is smeared beneath my eye so I look like a raccoon.

"No. No, no, no, no, no."

Maybe if I deny this hard enough, reality will warp and change. I'll be ready and calm when Darius arrives, with perfect make up and contacts and a wide smile, and the sight of me will blow his mind. Like in those teen movies, when the nerdy girl finally takes off her glasses. After one look at my red velvet dress—oh god, how did I ever think I could pull that off?—and my glossy auburn waves, he'll fall in love on the spot. He'll drop to one knee and propose, right there in my apartment hallway.

But, nope. No such luck. Life doesn't work that way, and when a knock rattles my front door, I'm still pressing a tissue to my eye and stumbling around barefoot.

82

"Shit." Half-blinded by my Kleenex, I stub my toe on the coffee table on my way to the door. Pain blooms in my foot, hot and sharp. "Ow! Shit!"

"Lucy?" That deep, smooth voice floats through my door. The voice that haunts my dreams. "Are you okay in there?"

"No!"

Darius jiggles the door handle, but it's locked. And I can't leave him out there in the hallway; can't pretend I haven't failed horribly at this date already. My toe throbs as I limp to the front door and undo the chain.

"Oh," Darius says when the door swings wide, gaze flicking over me. "Oh dear."

I burst into tears.

Darius curses, crowds me into the apartment, and shuts the door. And I hate that he's seeing me like this—red-face and snotty, with a stubbed toe and ruined makeup—but a calming voice whispers in my head that this isn't a *real* date. This doesn't *really* matter.

I had no chance with Darius Amin in the first place, so I haven't lost anything with this shit show—just embarrassed myself. Fine. That's what friends are for, right?

"Is it broken?" The composer shepherds me to the sofa, nudging me to sit down. "Luce, your toe. Does it feel broken?"

How can you tell? Gritting my teeth, I give my toes an experimental wiggle—and though the pain throbs, it doesn't feel any worse.

"N-no." I sniff, transferring the tissue from my eye to my nose. "I don't think so. It just hurts." Darius sees the mess of mascara, but like a champ, he doesn't comment. He's too busy rubbing my shoulders, stroking my arms, soothing me as he looms above the sofa, dressed like a movie star on a red carpet.

Life is cruel.

Here I am: a complete mess, barely keeping it together, already tortured with nerves. And there *he* is, looking like the front page of a glossy magazine.

His dark hair is styled, his jaw freshly shaved. That eggplant colored suit hugs Darius's sculpted body, and the crisp white shirt glows next to his smooth, bronze skin.

And he smells *good*. Woodsy and expensive.

Whatever his cologne is, I want to spray it on my pillow.

"So." My tear-stained face twists as Darius kneels on my rug, taking my foot in careful hands. He inspects my toes carefully, his touch so warm and gentle, and my voice quavers. "How am I doing on this practice date so far? Any notes?"

"No notes." Darius's smile is faint, his attention fixed on my toes. "It's the perfect amount of hysteria. You nailed it."

"Thank you. I tried."

And with his calming presence, the nerves are fading fast. My heartbeat slows, my tears dry up, and even the ache in my foot starts to ease. Darius is magic like that.

The snort comes out of nowhere. I press my lips together, fighting hard, but the giggles can't be stopped. They spill out of me, my shoulders shaking and my cheeks hot. Darius quirks a smile, still kneeling on my rug, and places my foot carefully down.

"You have an odd sense of humor."

"Yeah, well." My cheeks ache from fighting this grin. "It's either laugh or cry, right? And I already tried crying."

"True."

When Darius pushes to his feet, my breath catches, the giggles stalling in my throat. He tugs on his suit jacket and eyes my dress, my hair, my blotchy cheeks. The whole damn mess of me, sprawled on my sofa for his consideration.

Feeling those brown eyes on me... my body perks to life, even though I've surely never been less sexy.

The composer tilts his head. "Do you still want to go to the party?"

Doesn't *he*? Oh god, will I embarrass him too much?

"Um. Well. Do you?"

"Yes," Darius says immediately. "But only if you want to."

Whew. Okay.

"I do. But I need five minutes to redo my makeup and change my contacts, and I need to find a different dress—"

"Keep the dress." Taking my hand, Darius pulls me gently to my feet. Not even a whisper of pain now. "You'll break my heart if you change. Other than that, take as long as you need."

My head spins, both from his compliment and his hand on mine. "Shouldn't I be quick, though? Like on a real date?"

But Darius shakes his head, expression sour. "Any man worth dating won't rush you, Lucy."

Noted.

I still scurry to my bedroom extra fast. No need to keep my friend waiting.

* * *

"Let me split this with you."

We're tucked in the back of a cab, drifting through the city streets to the party. The night sky is dark, but so many lights glow all around that it's almost as bright as during the day.

Headlights. Lit-up windows. Glowing neon shop signs, and flickering advertisements on giant billboards. It all washes the streets in a bright electric glow, and I'm relieved to huddle in the shade of the cab.

"No."

Darius sits next to me, his elegant body folded into the leather seat. Sometime in the last few minutes, he snagged my wrist, and now he's tracing feather-light circles over my racing pulse point. It's hard to read his expression in the gloom.

But the wrist thing—it's all fake. For our practice date.

Yet goosebumps still ripple down my bare arms.

Red velvet clings to the rest of my body, hugging the hourglass shape of my curves—and my cheeks go hot every time I think about Darius demanding that I keep this dress on. Which, so far in the last fifteen minutes, has replayed in my mind about a billion times.

He really likes it?

He thinks it looks good?

Shaking my head, I try to focus: numbers. Cab fare. Right.

"We should split this, Darius." He's not budging, but I try again. "We're both benefiting from the ride, and actually you live closer to the party than I do, so really if anything, *I* should—"

"It's a date, Lucy." Darius fixes me with a look, that fingertip still swooping over my wrist. "Let me pay for you, woman. Stop fighting this."

"But—"

"I'm going to buy your drinks, too. Might as well make your peace with that now."

Ugh. Does he have to be so bossy about it? Such a caveman?

Although… a tiny, shameful, bad-feminist part of me loves this. Loves being treated like someone special. It feels so *nice*. Even if it's fake, even if it's all just practice, I've never had someone rush to pay for me before. Usually I'm the one bailing people out, then writing off their debt after a while when they've clearly forgotten.

…But not with Darius. Now that I think about it, whenever we go out for a friendly dinner together, we always fight to pay the bill, and he agrees that I'll pay it next time, but 'next time' never comes. Then there are those morning coffees and pastries, those treats that he never accepts payment for, even though I offer…

Oh, god. Am I a leech?

"I *want* to pay, Lucy." It's like Darius is reading my mind, studying the stiff set of my shoulders. Hearing all my unspoken doubts, and soothing them away with his circling thumb. "I love paying for you. Please let me. All I want is to take care of you."

I swallow, unsure, though my heart's pumping extra hard. He didn't mean anything by that. He means he loves taking care of me as his friend.

"I just—I feel like I'm taking advantage of you. Not only tonight, but those morning pastries… those dinners…. I feel terrible."

Darius inhales sharply, and raises my wrist to his mouth. The brush of his lips scorches all the way down to my toes, and his hot words tickle my skin.

"Don't take those things away from me, sweetheart. I love treating you. It's the best part of my day."

God. He shouldn't say things like that to me. It'll warp my brain and give me false hope. And I should argue more, but—

Can't think with Darius kissing my wrist.

Can't focus when the cab smells like his clean, manly skin.

Can't do anything except breathe shaky breaths, and squirm against my leather seat, and fight to ignore the tickle between my legs.

Just. Friends.

"Surrender," Darius growls, the hot flick of his tongue making my eyes cross. "Admit defeat, Lucy. Say you'll let me keep paying. Give in to me."

And he's half-teasing, half-serious, but I am one hundred percent cooked. My words are strangled when they burst out of me, and I'm lucky I can still string a sentence together, because my thoughts are so muddled. "Fine, you madman! Fine."

Darius winks in the darkness, pressing one last kiss to my wrist before lowering it to his lap. He doesn't release my arm, but goes back to drawing soft circles. Yeesh.

How long is this cab ride?

Will I even make it there with my sanity intact?

Or will I have gone mad with confused longing by then? Falling steadily more and more in love with my fake-date friend.

Darius

There is no way Leo planned a single detail about this party. I call bullshit. Because the man I know better than I know myself, the man who has been my rock since freshman year of college, does not *decorate*. No way.

And yet his skyscraper rooftop glitters with string lights, and a white gazebo covers the band on their small stage. As we step out onto the roof, my hand resting on Lucy's back, I count three pop-up cocktail bars and at least a dozen servers weaving through the crowd with trays of canapes.

"Nice work, Hazel." I wink at the boss's assistant where she stands by his side, greeting the guests as they arrive. And Hazel beams at me, but both Leo and Lucy stiffen at our exchange.

What? Why? What did I say?

Hazel *has* done a great job—and we all know this party was one hundred percent her. She's Leo's best employee, his right-hand woman. His blonde, perky General with a bright smile. Without her, he'd be even more grouchy and impossible, and that is saying something.

"Yes, thank you so much for tonight," Lucy says, stepping carefully away from my touch. Squeezing my hand into a fist, I keep my smile fixed in place. "And thank you, of course, Mr Corbin. It's so kind of you to throw us this party."

Leo grunts.

And he's never going to win the Mr Congeniality award, but Leo is grumpier than usual when he fixes me with a scowl, ignoring Lucy completely. "So much for keeping your distance, Amin."

My pulse races, even as I shrug at my oldest friend, cool as a cucumber. "It's just one night. No harm done."

"What are you talking about?" Hazel pipes up, and Lucy's frowning between us too. She shuffles another inch away from me, suspicion turning down her mouth, and Christ, I want to yank her back.

Want to bury my face in her throat and inhale.

Want to press her perfect, soft body against my front.

Want to twirl her around the dance floor and feed her chocolate-dipped strawberries and lick droplets of champagne off her wrist. Is that so wrong?

Not fit for love.

Not fit for love.

Right.

"Nothing." Leo glances down at his ball-of-sunshine assistant, and his scowl softens the tiniest amount. Ha! Such a hypocrite. "Would you like a drink?"

"Oh, of course!" Hazel tucks a clipboard under her arm and plucks his empty glass, oblivious to his unhappy frown. Guess I'm not the only would-be provider. "I'll fetch us some now. You stay here and greet everyone, and remember to smile!"

As her blonde ponytail whips away in the crowd, Leo sighs

and turns to me. "Not a word."

I mime zipping my lips closed, then take Lucy's hand. She lets me, thank god.

"See you on the other side, boss."

* * *

"What did Mr Corbin mean by that? When he said about keeping your distance?"

Two hours of dancing, chatting, and sniping canapes from servers' trays later, Lucy finally voices the question that has been chewing on her mind.

It's been bothering her. Doesn't take a detective to notice. When Lucy is preoccupied, she gets this little pinch in her eyebrows and she nibbles on her plump bottom lip.

It's been sweet torture, watching those pearly white teeth sink into her pillowy lip. So I've been waiting impatiently, my chest tight, for her to ask the question that will sink this whole night.

Because this isn't *practice*. This isn't fake—not to me.

I mean every dance, every teasing whisper, every time I tuck her hair behind her ear. Every drink I bring Lucy is an offering from my heart.

Rusty, useless heart though it may be.

So when Lucy finally asks, my stomach churns with dread. This is it. And I won't lie to her, but... perhaps this night can last a little longer before the sweet, shy accountant demands to go home and never wants to see me again.

"First, let's run through your lessons so far." It's easy to take Lucy's elbow and tug her gently into the crowd, nudging a path to the center of the dance floor. The breeze is strong this high

91

up on the rooftop, ruffling skirts and teasing the guests' hair, but I'm overheating under my suit. Hours with Lucy have me permanently flushed. "Lesson one. Dancing."

Lucy rolls her eyes but twines her arms around my neck—and god, this feels good. If I had my way, this particular lesson would never end.

The soft warmth of her body, pressed against mine. The way her generous curves mold to my chest, and the tickle of her hair against my neck. The floral scent of her skin, and the stars reflected in her green eyes. Everything.

"You know, of all the confusing parts of a first date, I think I can manage turning in a circle, Darius."

She *says* that, but when another guest brushes too close behind her, Lucy huddles against my chest. And I fucking love that—love being her safe harbor. Shooting a warning look over her shoulder, I gather her close, never wanting to let go.

"Alright, my beautiful know-it-all. Lesson two: flirting. Show me what you've learned."

And Lucy huffs, her warm breath tickling my throat, but she slides one palm into the center of my chest. The first two buttons of my shirt are undone, and her fingertip ghosts over the third button, then slips under the fabric to tease my bare skin.

It's the softest touch. Barely there at all.

And blood surges to my cock.

"It's hard to flirt on command," Lucy grouses, like she hasn't already earned an A+. That tiny point of contact from her fingertip on my bare chest—it's killing me. My body is coiling tight, muscles tensing on my bones, like I'm about to throw her over my shoulder and carry her into the shadows. If we weren't surrounded by our coworkers, maybe I would. "And not all of us are massive flirts like you, Darius. We can't all wink and have people fall at our feet."

"What are you talking about?" It's so hard to focus with Lucy crushed against me like this. The music is slow, sultry, and the chatter of the crowd floats up to the night sky.

"Hazel," Lucy mutters.

Wait. What?

"Hazel?"

The pinch between Lucy's eyebrows deepens to a full-on frown, and she looks tired suddenly. Bitter. And I keep turning her slowly, keep her gathered to my chest, but I'd give anything to kiss away that frown.

First, though, I need to understand whatever the hell is going on.

"Hazel?" I repeat. "Care to explain?"

"You *winked* at her earlier." A blush climbs Lucy's throat, and no, I will not lick it. This is a serious conversation. "When we first arrived. Just like you smile at the interns and they all swoon into a pile."

I bite back a laugh. "That's hardly what happens. You're exaggerating. And I'm not flirting with any of them, Luce, I'm just being friendly."

She scoffs. "Yeah, right."

"It's true." Christ, I wish she'd believe me on this. Because, okay, I *know* what I look like. I'm not an idiot: I know the effect I can have. My ruined, useless heart has an appealing wrapper. But does that mean I should be rude and dismissive with every person I meet? Shouldn't I still be friendly and kind?

I'm not Leo, damn it. My face isn't set in a permanent glower. My natural inclination is to smile, to make people feel comfortable, but that's not an invitation to more.

"You'd know if I was flirting, Luce."

Another scowl at my shirt collar. "Would I?"

"Yes. Because it would only ever be aimed at you."

There's a long, loaded pause between us, and we fill it by dancing in silence, spinning beneath the stars. String lights glitter all around us, and the band breaks into another slow song. After a while, Lucy puffs out a strained breath, then slips more of her fingertip beneath my shirt, pressing harder against my heated chest.

Yes.

"Lesson three," I grate out, heart thumping against that small point of contact. "Kissing."

Lucy jolts, that blush flooding her cheeks, and the look she gives me is so wary. "You haven't said anything about kissing."

"Haven't I?" Cupping her cheek slowly, I give her time to move away. "Maybe it's better if I show you."

The world tilts as I lower my head. And I'm going slowly, so slowly, dreading the inevitable moment when Lucy shoves me away, but then our lips brush—and my heart stops.

One second.

Two.

There's nothing but stunned silence in my chest.

Then finally, as I kiss her again, deeper this time, my poor heart jolts back to life, racing extra fast to catch up.

"*Mmph*," Lucy says against my lips, gripping the lapels of my jacket, tugging me closer.

Her lips are warm and plush, and her mouth tastes like the berry-flavored cocktail I brought her thirty minutes ago. Lucy opens for me on a sigh, her tongue nudging mine, and heat crackles down my spine.

My gut is clenched, and I'm harder than granite.

More.

I need more of this woman. Something tells me I'll never get enough.

Lucy's breath hitches when I deepen the kiss even further, our tongues sliding together. She's pressed completely against me now. Sealed tight, kissing me back, even as whispers drift around us on the dance floor.

...Darius Amin...

...Isn't that the girl from Accounts?...

...Lily or something...

This isn't right. It's Lucy's first kiss. She deserves privacy, not a bunch of gossips misremembering her name.

Gut swooping, I tear my mouth away, straighten up and stare blindly out at the crowd. Lucy's breathing hard too, still squeezing my lapels in her hands, and it takes a moment for my brain to come back online. For me to register what I'm seeing.

Leo leans against the band's gazebo, his arms folded and expression stony.

Leo Corbin watches me. Judges me as I break my promise.

"...need some air?"

Lucy's words filter through the chaos in my brain, and I glance down with a blink. "What?"

She flinches, taking her hands away. "I asked if you needed some air. You look pale."

"I'm..."

Wrecked. Ruined. A liar and a hopeless excuse for a friend.

Shaking my head, I force my brain back into gear. "I'm fine. There you go, Luce. There's lesson three."

Her lips press together. Green eyes watch me closely, her pupils still blown from our kiss. "A lesson? Is that still what this is, Darius? Practice?"

Leo's gaze bores into me from afar, making my neck itch. He looks so pissed off at me. So disappointed.

And he's right. He *should* be. Because didn't I say I'd keep my distance? Didn't I promise to stay away from this girl? And here I am twirling her around a dance floor, flirting and stealing kisses, hiding behind the excuse of 'practice' while Lucy deserves a man who can be what she needs.

Whole. Functional. A man who knows what a healthy relationship looks like; a man who can do this thing right.

"Darius," Lucy presses, and she sounds so strained. Damn. I aim a smile at her, but it feels wrong on my face.

"Of course this is still practice," I say. "But it's fun practice, right?"

"Fun," Lucy repeats. Her shoulders slump. "I see."

And I'm mentally patting myself on the back, congratulating myself for dodging the awkward questions and smoothing this over, when Lucy turns on her heel and marches away without another word. The crowd parts for her and swallows her whole, her red velvet dress blocked by dark suits and flowing skirts, and I'm left gaping after her on the dance floor.

My heart gives a sickly lurch.

"Lucy!" I call.

Heads turn, but none of them have her auburn waves.

"Luce!"

The band finishes one song, and in the lull before they start another, I hear the whispers all around me. The gossipy murmurs, swarming like bees, until my face is hot and my stomach is tight and I hate every single person on this rooftop except one.

Why can't they leave me the hell alone? Why can't they all

mind their own business? It's the rumors they spread, the gossip about me, which makes Lucy think I'm sleeping with half the interns. No one here really knows me except Leo—and he thinks the worst of me. Thinks I'm doomed to screw this up, because *he* can't let himself love. Can't admit to wanting more.

Cursing under my breath, I shoulder my way through the dancing couples. Fuck that. Fuck this.

I need my sweet accountant.

Lucy

꧁ꙮ꧂

It's louder down on the street, cars rumbling past the sidewalk as drivers lean on their horns. It rained for an hour or so earlier, and the ground is black and shiny, reflecting their headlights. Tires swish through shallow puddles.

Huddled in the doorway out of the way of the pedestrians, I fumble with my phone, trying to keep it together long enough to order a ride home.

It's ridiculous that Darius's words should make me lose control like this—that every time I replay them, it feels like being stabbed.

Practice. That's all he ever promised me from tonight.

And practice is what he gave me.

So why do I feel sick with betrayal? Why do I want to headbutt his stupid, handsome face? Why is my chest a smoking crater underneath my dress?

Finally, I find the app I need. Browsing for nearby drivers, I clench my jaw against the threat of tears.

I will not cry here.

I will not sob out my broken heart in the street below my office party.

I will make it home, change into flannel pajamas, and *then* fall apart like a grown up, damn it.

Ride confirmed. Tracking the little dot of my savior on the map, I stare dry-eyed as my driver inches through traffic.

That was my first kiss.

My *only* kiss.

Darius took that from me, and it didn't even mean anything to him. Is that allowed? Is that what I agreed to with this fake date? Am I an idiot?

"Lucy."

Normally, the deep, smooth sound of Darius Amin's voice makes butterflies explode inside me. Right now, it makes my teeth grind.

"Lucy," he says, coming to my side. Didn't hear the front door open, or I would have made a run for it, even in these heels. "There you are. Please, don't leave like this."

The *really* messed up thing is that Darius sounds as wrecked as I feel. Like tonight is an emotional rollercoaster for him too, but that makes no sense.

He's the heartthrob who sees me as a friend, nothing more. This is all a big joke to him.

I'm the dumbass on a fake date with her crush.

And when I put it like that, I can't even be mad at him. Not really. Darius hasn't done anything that I didn't agree to— eagerly.

"Just a headache," I mutter, tilting my phone so he can see my ride is nearly here. Darius snakes a hand out faster than I can react, canceling my ride with the tap of a button. "Hey!"

"Don't lie to me, Lucy." Great. Now he's pissed off, too—and when I finally look up, Darius is rumpled and angry, his normally smooth appearance fraying. "You can feel however you need to feel, but don't lie to me, damn it. Not me."

But I *do* have a headache. It's called Darius Amin.

And there's a simple cure: a ride home, alone, and then a pint of butterscotch ice cream on my sofa. This treatment is tried and tested, okay? Because this is not my first rodeo. Not my first meltdown about loving the man in front of me—it's just the first one that he's seen.

"Come back upstairs," he begs.

I snatch my phone back. "Hard pass."

"Not to the party. I—there's somewhere else we can go. Somewhere to talk this out. Then I swear, I will get you home safely and leave you be, just… please, Lucy." Those mournful brown eyes bore into my *soul.* "Don't leave things broken between us. I can't bear it."

And *I* can't bear to see this man crumbling with despair. Because he's not just my heart-stoppingly handsome crush, after all—he's my friend.

My infuriating, charming, caring friend. The man who brings me coffee and pastries every morning. Crap. I owe him more than this, don't I?

"Ten minutes." That's all I can handle. I shove my phone in my clutch, already counting down. "Then I'm gone. I really do have a headache."

"Ten minutes," Darius agrees quickly. "Deal."

He leads me back into the building, across the fancy marble lobby, and into the elevator. The doorman waves us off as the doors close.

And we lift off, carried up to where another painful conversation awaits. I swear to god: this night is eternal.

* * *

The elevator stops just below the roof. "The penthouse?" I say stupidly, tripping out after Darius as he leads us to the only door in the short corridor. The floor tiles, the light fixtures, the sage-green walls—everything here seems fancy and expensive. It's a far cry from my own sixth floor walk-up, with my threadbare curtains and constantly humming refrigerator. "Why are we *here*?"

"Got a key." Darius fishes a bunch from his pocket, jingling them at me with a brisk smile—but it doesn't reach his eyes. He was silent in the elevator too, the air thick between us. "A spare. The boss won't care if we borrow his place for ten minutes."

The *boss*?

Darius ignores my squeak of protest, tugging me inside the penthouse. My heels clack against oak floorboards, and my dress swishes around my legs.

"We can't—we shouldn't—"

"Oh, calm down. It's just some light breaking and entering. Leo would never press charges, so don't worry. He's the one who cut me the key."

Gaping at the back of Darius's broad shoulders, the door swinging shut behind me, I trail him into an open plan kitchen and living area. Who *is* this man? He's close with the boss? Why didn't I know that?

When I voice the question, Darius shoots me a bitter smile from the open refrigerator. "Maybe you don't know me as well as you think you do, Luce."

Huh.

101

Okay, need a minute to process. I peer around the apartment—*Leo Corbin's* apartment. It's less of a cold bachelor pad than I expected, with vibrant art on the walls and a comfy-looking teal sofa. There's one of those fancy fireplaces too, the ones with a remote control.

Meanwhile, Darius is rummaging for something, lit by the refrigerator's glow. Bottles clink together, and the composer moves like he's been here a million times before. Like this is a second home to him.

Shoot. Maybe I *don't* know him as well as I think.

Like—the flirting thing. I was so sure that when he winked at Hazel it was flirty, but... she didn't blush. She didn't seem to think so. So why leap to the worst conclusion?

And sure, there are countless rumors about Darius sleeping with women in the company, but have I ever actually heard of him going on a date? Have any of those rumors been confirmed? Not one. And I'd hate it if Darius believed a bunch of baseless rumors about me.

Chewing my bottom lip, I wander to a floor lamp and flick it on. No need to hash this out in half-darkness.

Over in the kitchen, Darius straightens with a bottle of white wine in his hand. It's been opened and re-corked, and the label says it's fancy stuff.

"We can't drink the boss's wine," I hiss, already mortified but so, so tempted. The shame and heartbreak of earlier is receding, fading into the background, and now I've got that fizzy, excited feeling. The tingles that come with breaking the rules.

And Capable, Reliable Lucy *never* breaks the rules. She's always punctual and hardworking, dressed in forgettable cardigans and glasses, blending in with the furniture. That's how I've seen myself recently, anyway.

But when Darius strolls to meet me, two glasses of white wine in his hands, his heated gaze says he sees me very, very differently. His mouth crooks. "Go on. Live a little."

Holding my breath, I take a glass.

It's cool, the pale wine sparkling in the light when I swill it gently. My first sip is crisp and sweet. Darius switches the fireplace on with a beep, tossing the remote who knows where as flames leap to life in the grate.

And... is this a seduction? With the wine, the fire, and the glittering city-scape outside the window, it kinda feels like a seduction.

But that's wishful thinking. *Practice*, he said.

And we're here to finish our argument, not to extend our fake date. Still, the devil on my shoulder makes me blurt my next question.

"Is this the part where you whisper sweet nothings in my ear?" I'm aiming for jokey, but it's coming out strained. "Where you kiss my neck and pull me down to the rug, and ravish me until I cry out your name?"

Darius frowns down at his own wine, refusing to meet my eye. "It depends. Would you let me?"

Yes.

Even if it meant nothing, yes. Even if it broke my heart, and ruined me for other men for the rest of my life, yes I would. What does that say about me? Does it make me passionate or stupid?

Capable, Reliable Lucy would never hook up in her boss's penthouse. But then, that girl believed the rumors and thought the worst about her friend; she decided Darius Amin could never possibly want her without even asking him first.

Maybe I don't want to be that girl anymore.

Maybe I want to be Brave Lucy. Reckless Lucy.

The Lucy who goes after what she wants. The Lucy who sips delicious stolen wine.

"Well, I'd prefer the sofa," I say.

Darius huffs a laugh, and when he smiles up at me, his eyes crinkle. "We should talk first. You seemed upset."

I was. I *am*.

But there is such a thing as multitasking. We can talk things through *and* despoil the boss's apartment.

So with one final sip of wine, I wander to the mantelpiece and set my glass down. The fire blasts heat against my bare legs, and when I turn back to Darius, my spine is straight.

"I was hurt." No more dancing around it; no more half-lies. No more hiding how I feel from the man I want most in the world, because all this secrecy is killing me. Better to be honest and rejected than to wonder *what if*. "You took my first kiss and it didn't mean anything to you. That pissed me off. Especially because… well, it didn't feel like practice."

"It wasn't." Darius shakes his head, then strides to join me at the mantelpiece. His glass is placed beside mine with a *click*. And his back is straight too, like we've both been carrying these heavy loads and we're finally setting them down. "I've been such an ass, Lucy, letting my fears get in the way. None of it was fake to me. None of it. Of course that kiss meant something to me—it meant the world."

My whole body tightens, quivering with hope.

"Then why—?"

"I could never deserve you." A strong hand curves around my hip, searing me through my red velvet dress. I'm falling into those steady brown eyes. "I have no idea how to do any

104

of this. My parents hated each other and put me off the idea of love for years; my best friend from college is a determined loner. I've never seen a happy couple up close, never learned how it's done."

Darius's mouth twists, and turmoil swirls in those dark eyes. Jeez, he's really worried about this, isn't he? This has really kept him away from me for a year.

Men. Honestly.

"Darius." He inhales sharply when I take his hand, my thumb rubbing back and forth on his palm. "Maybe I'm not the only one who needs practice."

The composer chokes out a laugh, like he can't believe this is real.

"You'd do that for me? Figure things out as we go?"

And oh, this beautiful dumbass. Fighting a smile, I place my other hand on his chest, slipping my fingertip beneath his shirt again. "Obviously. How do you think everyone else does it? Do you think there's a secret manual?"

Darius hums, head lowering. "No?"

Our breath mingles, and we're a hair's breadth away from kissing. My second ever kiss. "Good instinct. So we can figure it out, right? We're smart people."

"*You're* smart people." Darius nips my bottom lip. "I'm all looks, sweetheart."

And he's teasing me again, hands roaming, breathing faster, but when our mouths meet, all is right with the world.

Fight? What fight?

And what fake date?

Turns out neither of us are good actors, because we meant every heated look, every dance, every touch. Both of us pretended it wasn't real while dying on the inside, contorted with longing. What a pair we are.

"There will be rumors on Monday." Tugging his jacket off his broad shoulders, I kiss Darius again and again until my head spins. He kisses me back, devouring my mouth, my neck, my jaw. "Everyone will be gossiping about you again."

"Good." The jacket lands with a soft thump somewhere behind the sofa. "Let them. They've finally stumbled on something true."

And… *the* Darius Amin, famous composer, with the bookish accountant with glasses? Will anyone even believe it? Will they think it's too ridiculous? Will they—

No.

Not going down that path.

I don't care how it looks to everyone else in the office. Don't care if they think Darius is too handsome for me. Because the fact is *he* wants me—so desperately that he's growling, popping a button off his shirt as he tears it open—and that's all that matters. Everyone else can kick rocks.

"So," Darius says between kisses, squeezing my waist, my hips, my ass, "fucking… sweet. *Lucy*. You know how long I've wanted this?"

I laugh as he kisses down my throat, raking my fingers through his hair. It's thick and soft and springy, and it smells like cedar wood and lime. "A year?"

A growl rumbles against my skin. "Longer. Much longer. From the first fucking second I laid eyes on you, walking across the lobby in your fussy little pencil skirt, I wanted to—"

"Yeah?"

Clever fingers stroke over my back, searching for the entrance to my dress. Grabbing Darius's arm, I redirect him to my side, sucking in a quick breath when he starts tugging the zipper.

"*Yes.*" His mouth finds mine again, claiming, *devouring*. His tongue strokes against mine, and I'm burning up in my skin, burning to a crisp, panting and swaying in the composer's arms.

My *friend's* arms.

And now so much more.

"Wanted to tear that cardigan right off you." The zipper catches, and Darius yanks it on with a snarl. Jeez, I've never seen him like this—half-feral, with a ravenous glint in his dark eyes. Gone is the calm, collected man from the office, and here instead is a man whose control has frayed to the last thread. "Wanted to drag you into that supply closet and shake the walls."

Oh, crap.

I'd let him.

I'd totally let him.

And now we're tearing our clothes off in the boss's penthouse, our work party happening above our heads, and the fire is hot and my bare skin is pebbled with goosebumps. If we stop, I might die.

Darius steers me to the sofa and coaxes me to sit down. To stretch out, legs parted, thighs quivering.

"This," he says, thudding to his knees on the rug. Warm hands cup my knees. "*This*. This is my dream."

And it's all a perfect whirl: his bare, sculpted body, the dark hair dusting his chest and drawing a line down his abs, the lamplight, his touch, his breath, the tickle of his hair as his head lowers between my legs.

Darius Amin pauses, brown gaze searching. His cheeks are flushed. "Yes?"

And I'm already squirming, the backs of my knees sweaty with how badly I need this. "*Yes.*"

His head ducks.

Firelight glimmers in the dark strands of his hair. His breath puffs against my bare seam, tickly and warm, and then—

Heat.

Wet, torturous heat.

A flattened tongue licks the length of my slit.

He *laves* me, licking and sucking and nibbling everywhere, exploring every inch. And my breaths come in short pants, my fingers twisting in his hair, because that's *Darius* down there, tasting me so intimately. That's Darius Amin sliding a finger inside me, crooking it to tease my inner walls. That's Darius torturing me into a sweaty, babbling heap.

My hips rock up to meet his mouth. My squishy thighs grip his ears. Is he okay? Does he *like* this? Is it—

"Luce," Darius groans, his words vibrating against my clit. "You taste so fucking good. Give it to me, sweetheart. Give me everything. Rub yourself on my tongue."

Oookay.

You know, I've always been an A+ student. Always been good at following instructions.

And if Darius wants me to let loose, to surrender to this completely... I sure will.

With a sigh, I melt back against the sofa, even as my hands tug him closer by the hair, yanking his face harder between my legs. Darius rumbles his approval, mouth working furiously between my thighs.

The wave builds slowly at first, then faster and faster, until I can't hold it back any longer, can't keep it from cresting. My heart thuds and my cheeks flush and my eyes screw shut, anguished breaths echoing in my ears.

"Oh!"

Lucy

It crashes over me, trembling my whole body. On and on it goes, until I'm a boneless heap, sprawled naked on my boss's teal sofa.

Darius sits back on his heels, and his mouth and chin are slick in the firelight.

"Lucy?"

I wobble up to look at him properly. "Uh-huh?"

His gaze burns. "You're *mine*."

Darius

"**Y**ou're *mine*."

The words punch out of my chest, throbbing with possession. And I know it's too much, too fast, it surely wouldn't be in any How To manual, but I don't care. This is a law of nature.

Lucy is *mine*, she always has been and always will be, and I'm going to spend the rest of our lives convincing her of that fact. Showing her, through my actions and words, that I'm not a bad bet. I *can* love, and love right, because I'm already turned inside out over her. I'll do this right.

She's rewritten my DNA.

She's burned into my blood.

And right now, her sweet, salty tang is on my tongue.

Best thing I've ever tasted. Who needs food? Whenever I get hungry from now on, I'll burrow under Lucy's skirt—especially if it gives her that glazed, blissed-out look. So beautiful.

Never seen her so relaxed. My Lucy is normally so uptight and tense, keeping everything running smoothly in the background, always crucial but never really thanked. Her To Do list is a mile long, and it plays in stressful loops in her brain.

Now, though, she's turned to jelly. A pink flush stains her gorgeous chest, and her smile is dreamy. "I'm yours, huh?"

All. Mine.

She won't regret it, I swear. Screw those fears. Now that I've found the center of my universe, now that I've surrendered to this, I'm ready to orbit around her, meeting her needs, building up her confidence. Bringing out the vixen I know is hidden inside those cardigans.

Not that I want to change her clothes.

In fact, next time we do this, I want her wearing those glasses. The cute little tortoiseshell ones that make her look like a librarian.

Christ. Gripping my shaft, I jerk myself once. Twice.

I'm so hard I could drill through concrete.

Want to keep going. Want to claim her fully. Want to thrust and rut and paint her insides, but I'll never push this woman faster than she's ready. Will never make her feel pressured. I'd rather die, I'd rather throw myself off a cliff—

"Darius," Lucy says, reaching for me, smiling that well-pleasured smile. "Come here."

She guides me on top of her, stretching longer on the sofa. Lets me lower my bare body on top of hers, hooking her ankles around the back of my calves.

"I'm yours," she says again, feathering kisses over my jaw. My gut swoops, and my cock is so hard it vibrates. "So prove it. Take what you want."

What I *want* is Lucy in my bed every morning, with my ring on her finger.

I want her sleepy Sunday smiles, and to bring her coffee

and pastries in bed, and I want to bicker over the crossword together.

But, okay: I definitely want this too. When my shaft glides over her slick folds, coating the head in her wetness, my heart thumps hard enough to bruise.

"We don't have to…"

"I want to." Lucy nuzzles my throat, humming, and Christ, that's the best thing I've ever felt. Memory bank hall of fame. "If you want to, I do too."

Ha!

What a question. As if my gut is not already cramping with the need to be inside her.

"I'm going to be good to you." My muscles shake as I lower down, rocking harder against her. Getting good and slick. But I'm not shaking because I'm tired, not with all this adrenaline coursing through my system—no, I'm nervous. This is it.

"Don't listen to the gossips, Luce. I'm going to love you so fucking much that we'll be a boring married couple to them. They'll lose interest in us completely, because we're so stupid in love with each other."

She laughs weakly, winding her arms around my neck. "I know."

When I nudge at her entrance, we both hold our breath.

And when I sink inside the first inch, we let out twin groans. So tight. So hot. So slick and hungry, sucking me deeper, even as her body strains to adjust. Lucy whimpers and keens and shifts beneath me on the sofa, her glossy hair spread over the cushions. Over in the fireplace, the flames pop and crackle.

"Tight," I mutter, sweat beading my forehead.

"Virgin," she says. "Remember?"

As if I could forget. And this is both a huge, life-changing gift and a hell of a lot of pressure, so my focus arrows down on Lucy's face as I thrust gently, working my way deeper.

I'll *never* hurt her. Not now, not ever.

But apparently Lucy has less patience than I do, because after several long, slow thrusts, she huffs and yanks me deeper with her heels. Her hips rock, and that blush spreads, and her eyes flutter half-closed.

Lucy's moans are the best thing I've ever heard.

Wedged halfway inside her, it feels like angels should be singing. Tooting hard on their heavenly trumpets, celebrating the best goddamn day of my life. Of *any* man's life.

Gritting my teeth, I press deeper.

In.

Out.

Slowly. Gently.

Letting her body adjust and her breaths get heavy. I work my girl open until she's rolling her hips up to meet mine, and I'm burrowing all the way deep with each thrust, teeth clacking together as the sofa creaks.

Poor Leo. I'll confess tomorrow and buy him new furniture. He'll probably change the locks, but it's worth it.

"Darius, I—*hngh.*"

I lick a stripe up Lucy's throat. Her skin is salty with sweat. Delicious.

Love when she says my name. Love when her eyes roll back and she loses her train of thought, too busy working herself on my shaft.

"D–Darius," she tries again, face creasing as I thrust harder, pounding her into the sofa cushions. "Shit. *Yes.* Like that. Just like that. Oh, god."

As my lady wishes.

Lucy is so perfect like this, shameless and wild. With her tits jiggling and her mouth swollen from my kisses, her eyes bright and hair mussed. No one else sees this side of her, only me, and that makes the beast in my chest roar in triumph.

"What are you trying to tell me, sweetheart?" Hooking her thigh higher, I change the angle, hitting a spot inside Lucy that makes her howl and claw at the cushions. "Go on, spit it out."

She glares, but her mouth twitches with humor, even now. God, I love teasing this woman—especially when she gets her revenge by clamping down on my length, squeezing me with her inner muscles until I nearly choke on my tongue.

"*Hngh*," I say.

"Spit it out, Darius."

Rallying, I snake a hand between us and thumb her clit. And when Lucy's head tips back, when her moan floats up to the ceiling, I know I've won this particular battle. "Tell me."

"I want you to…"

Lucy grunts, burying her face in my throat. And I keep thrusting, rubbing, chasing her higher, even as my back muscles tremble and sweat slides down my spine.

"Yes?"

"Want you to c—" Lucy breaks off, tossing her head, raking my chest with her nails. Little spitfire. "Want you to…to come in me. *Please*."

Holy hell.

My gut cramps, sparks zipping down my spine, and as my thumb rubs circles on her nub, I send up a silent prayer that I can last through this. That I can get her there first.

"You first, sweetheart." Tendons stand out in my neck, and I keep thrusting, plunging deep. "Come for me. Show me how pretty you are when you fall apart."

The answer: like a goddamn angel.

As though she was waiting for my command, Lucy tenses up, breath seizing. Her channel clamps down on me, twitching and tight, and I can't wait any longer. Wedging as deep as I can go, I follow my girl over the precipice. Soaring, flying, falling.

I'd follow her anywhere. To the ends of the Earth.

And when I pump her full, flooding her with spurt after spurt, my frantic heart finally settles in my chest. The beast inside me purrs.

Yes.

Lucy is mine. Claimed and filled until she drips.

About time.

* * *

One year later

It's eight AM on a Sunday, and that means I'm behind schedule. Power-walking down the sunlit street, with launderettes, cafes, and used bookstores passing in my peripheral vision, I clear my throat and walk faster.

There's no reason to stress like this. Not *really*. Lucy won't care if I bring coffee and pastries to her reading nook rather than waking her with a kiss on the forehead, but *I* care, damn it. I swore a private oath.

Besides, bringing my wife breakfast in bed is one of my great joys. And if there hadn't been an unexpected line at our favorite bakery, if some tourist hadn't spent forever umming and ahhing over custard tarts and bear claws, I'd already be home—picking flecks of pastry off Lucy's pajama top, rather than here, zooming around a young mother with a double-wide buggy.

It's a bright, warm day, and the air is crisp. Away from the city center, we actually get some quiet on Sunday mornings, broken only by the rumble of occasional passing cars and the *smack, bounce* of neighborhood kids playing basketball.

My chest throbs with the need to get home already. To see my wife, and deliver her special decaf coffee. To rub her feet, sore and swollen from her third trimester, and reassure her for the millionth time that she doesn't look like a hippo. That, frankly, I wouldn't care if she *did*.

Lucy is always beautiful to me.

Our building is quiet when I reach it, my steps echoing on the lobby tiles. There's an ancient elevator, but I hit the stairwell instead, because I can climb faster than that thing rises.

My paper bag crinkles. I've brought her almond croissants today, lightly dusted with icing sugar. The pastries seep warmth through the paper, clutched carefully to my chest.

Did Lucy sleep alright?

Did the baby kick and keep her awake?

Lucy, Lucy, Lucy.

My wife is always on my mind.

Our door is painted green, cheerful and bright. Sliding the key into the lock, I try to open it quietly.

"Darius?" a soft voice calls.

Damn. My heart sinks, but I let myself in properly and close the door behind me.

Our apartment is sunlit and cozy, with kitschy throws on the furniture and overflowing bookshelves. When I reach the living room, Lucy smiles at me from her favorite armchair, her feet propped on a footstool.

"Shit," I say, crossing to her and handing her the croissants and take out coffee. "I knew I was too late to wake you."

Her sweet laugh follows me into the kitchen as I fetch her a plate. "Oh yeah, shame on you, Darius. Bringing me breakfast like this every Sunday morning. What a jerk."

The burning sensation in my chest fades as I go back to her, turning to something warm and gooey. If Lucy's not disappointed, then it really is fine.

I'll still do better next week. Treat her right. And in the meantime, I lift her feet off the footstool then sit there, settling her heels in my lap.

Lucy moans, eyelids fluttering as she chews her almond croissant. Maybe from the foot rub, maybe from the pastry. Perhaps both.

"Hippo feet," she murmurs, crumbs dropping to her pajama shirt. There's icing on her top lip.

"*Perfect* feet." I nibble her big toe to prove it and Lucy squeals, trying to wriggle away.

Not happening.

Lucy is the center of my world, and she's *mine*.

And I'll spoil her for the rest of my days.

Tangling with the Boss

Description

~~~~~~~~~~~~~~~~~~

I tried to quit my job.

Now my grumpy boss won't let me out of his sight.

For the last four years, Leo Corbin has barely tolerated me. He rolls his eyes when I bring him homemade flapjacks; he grumbles when I chat his ear off in the elevator. He's made it clear, time and time again, that my perkiness is a problem he suffers through.

Then I hand in my resignation letter... and the boss loses his freaking mind.

Now he won't let me out of arm's length. Won't stop *fussing* over me, and giving me flowers and other gifts, and growling when other men get too close.

Jeez. Does he really want me to stay as his assistant this badly?

Or is Leo Corbin fighting for his wife?

Hazel

∽∾∽

Quitting this job is a last resort. Just to be clear. I don't take the amazing pay or the generous benefits for granted, and I *know* the people can't possibly be any nicer at my next office. Grapevine is as good as it gets.

But I can't stand it any longer. Can't go on this way. I'm weak, okay?

If I spend another year in love with the boss here, pining after him while he barely tolerates my presence, I'll go mad.

My fingers tremble as I fold my resignation letter, the paper still warm from the printer. Heartbeat thumping in my ears, I slide the letter inside a snowy white envelope.

It's fine. So fine! This is totally fine.

I'm not tucking my bleeding heart away in this envelope. Not losing a piece of myself. That's ridiculous.

But when Leo Corbin bellows for me from inside his office, that thunderous voice rattling the walls, I jump up with a squeak, my cheeks flaming. Like I'm doing something wrong out here, something sneaky.

"Hazel? Hazel! Get in here."

Seriously, why do I love this man? He's such an ogre sometimes. Huffing out a breath, I snatch up the envelope and edge around my desk, mentally rehearsing the moment that I'll give it to him.

Just place it on his desk and run away. Be a coward! That's why it's in writing, yeah?

We're on the top floor of this building, just the two of us alone up here. My desk is out in the| antechamber, where I can halt visitors and save Leo from ninety-nine percent of the conversations he would otherwise hate. His office, meanwhile, if you ever get a peek inside it, is all huge, sparkling windows and abstract paintings and views of the city stretching away in all directions. His fortress of solitude.

There's only one wall between us. Only one door.

But lately, it feels like a vast chasm. One that I can't get across, no matter how hard I try.

Because I desperately want to be welcome in that room—and preferably balanced on the boss's knee. But meanwhile, he sees me as just as much of a pest as everyone else, and it *hurts.* It makes my chest ache.

Hoo, boy. Okay. Tugging my purple dress straight and firming my shoulders, I rap on the boss's door.

"Come in," he rumbles, and I swear to god—the vibrations from his voice tingle through my feet. My palm is sweaty on the door handle, but I fumble it open and slip inside to where the ceiling is higher somehow, the sunlight brighter.

Leo watches me from beneath lowered eyebrows. His dark hair looks thick and tuggable; his eyes are piercing blue.

And he's scowling.

Always scowling at me.

124

"Everything ready for tonight?" Leo Corbin is a man of few words, and he leaps straight to the point. Shaking off my spiraling thoughts, I fix a bright smile on my face.

"Yes! Everything's ready. The caterers and the band will set up this afternoon."

He grunts again. That's Leo for 'good', though you wouldn't know it from his grumpy frown and firm jaw. If anyone ever gets this man to crack a smile, the fabric of reality might tear apart.

"Tonight needs to go well, Hazel." The boss rubs his jaw, glowering out of the window. "I'm not throwing another fucking party. This is it. Make it count."

"Roger that."

As if I'm half-assing this event! The Grapevine ten year anniversary party has haunted my freaking dreams for months. More than once, I've woken up sweating in the night, reciting guest lists and drink options. I've been *on* it. This event is my masterpiece.

But Leo doesn't care about that. If anything, he seems crankier than usual, slumped in his chair and tugging on his collar, so his morning meeting with our star composer must not have gone well. The way his shoulders bunch up is a dead giveaway. I can read this man's moods like a weather report.

And this is bad timing. The boss is rattled already.

But this envelope feels like it weighs one hundred pounds. I *need* to set it down. Need to get this over with.

"What's that?" Leo is doing that one-eyed squinty thing he does when he's got a headache brewing, and I'm already itching to run and fetch him a painkiller and a cool glass of water. Hate when he's in pain. But my feet are glued to the floorboards, my stomach twisting into knots as Leo drags the envelope across his desk and rips it open with a scowl. "You already brought the mail..."

He trails off, frown deepening as he reads.

Silence fills the office, swelling between us and cutting off my air supply.

Oh, god. Oh, *god*.

Can't breathe. Can't think.

And this is awful. Easily one of the top ten worst moments of my life, and I've had some doozies. In fifth grade, I tried to dye my blonde hair pink with a box kit and botched it so badly, half my hair fell out. Everyone at school called me Gollum.

"I'll work my notice period—"

Leo cuts off my squeaky voice. "You're not leaving, Hazel."

Well... I am. That's what my resignation letter says, right there in black ink. But sometimes the boss needs a minute to process bad news, so I suck in a huge breath and keep going. He'll catch up, and then he'll probably be glad.

No more perky assistant trying to cheer him up on gloomy mornings! No more elevator rides with me chatting his ear off about my weekend baking disasters! No more *me*!

Leo will see. This is for the best.

He'll get the serious, silent assistant of his dreams, and I'll get a chance to nurse my poor, bruised heart far away from his scowls.

"My new role starts on the fifteenth. If you would be willing to write me a reference before then, that would be—"

"New role?" Leo blinks and sits up straighter. His desk chair creaks under his impressive bulk. "You have a new job lined up? This is serious?"

Lord, give me patience. This man is experiencing a shock.

"Yes," I tell him gently. "I'm starting a new job on the

fifteenth."

He's already shaking his dark head. "No, you're not." His big hand twitches around my letter, crumpling it into a ball. "You're not leaving, Hazel. This is not happening."

When I burst out laughing, Leo looks at me like I've gone insane—and maybe I have. The jitters have taken over my body, and there's a weird ringing noise in my ears. None of this is going like I expected, but I have to push through, because the second I leave this room, my jelly legs will give out. I'll collapse into a sad puddle on the floor.

"You don't even like me, boss."

He blanches, shaking his head.

And I wait for the words to come—any words, anything nice at all, because if Leo asks me in this moment to stay, if he says he actually likes me, I'll do it. I'll cave.

But he gives me nothing. Nada. Zip.

The big, scary boss opens and closes his mouth like a goldfish. The man I'm desperately in love with can't deny that he finds me annoying.

Oof. New low.

And meanwhile, a crack splinters through my chest, pain searing my insides. See, this is why I'm leaving. It's self preservation, that's all, because I deserve to find a man who *likes* me. A man who's thrilled by my bouncy attitude and who can't get enough of my chatter. Hell, even just a boss who'll tolerate my presence without wincing.

So although this hurts even worse than I thought it would, although it feels like I'm sawing off a limb, I need to stay strong. Need to hold out for something healthier. Something *sweet*.

For starters: a man who sees me as more than a planner on legs. An *annoying* planner at that.

"You let me handle tonight's party." If we didn't have this giant desk between us, I'd pat Leo's shoulder. He looks shell-shocked. "You focus on that reference, okay? And I'll set up interviews for my replacement. Don't worry, I know your wish list by now: someone who won't speak unless they're spoken to, and who doesn't believe in Flapjack Fridays."

AKA: not me.

"Hazel," Leo says.

"And I know you hate interviewing, but I promise this will all be over in no time. The fifteenth will come so fast and then you'll forget I was ever here, I swear! This transition will happen in a blur."

"*Hazel.*" The boss sprawls back in his chair, breathing hard, face chalky-pale. If I didn't know better, I'd call for a doctor, because he looks *ill*. Does he really hate change that much? He coped okay when we repainted the lobby. "I mean it," he says. "You can't leave."

Master of the universe. That's who Leo Corbin is in this building; that's who he's been to me for the last four years. The all-powerful master of all he surveys... including me.

When he gives orders, we hop to it.

When he asks questions, we rush to answer.

No one tells him no. What Leo wants, he gets, and that conditioning is *strong*. It takes every ounce of my willpower to raise my chin and meet his gaze square-on.

"This is happening," I say, and if my voice is shaky as hell... it still counts as a victory. I'm standing my ground, damn it! I'm protecting my wrung-out heart! "I'm sorry, but it's not open for discussion. Some things aren't."

And it's not the best parting shot, but I turn on my heel anyway—because one more minute in this room will make me fray into a thousand pieces.

Leo

❧⟡❧

T he door clicks shut behind my assistant, and I stare at the handle with dry eyes. Waiting for it to jiggle. Waiting for Hazel to burst back in here and declare this is all a terrible joke—that this is the long-awaited sequel to the April Fool's Day cream tart made of shaving cream that she left on my desk last year. Yet another example of her god-awful sense of humor.

The clock ticks on the wall.

Swallowing hard, I wait.

But... nothing. The door handle is still, and there are no sounds from the next room. No muffled giggles as Hazel relays her prank on the phone, and no creak of floorboards as she eavesdrops outside the door.

Nothing. She's just... gone.

She dropped that bombshell, blew my goddamn life apart, then just... left.

Jesus Christ. Has she really found another job? Is that true?

Gusting out a ragged breath, I lurch to my feet and out

from behind my desk, then pace back and forth in front of the windows, wracking my brain to make sense of this. Trying to sort through the wreckage.

Back and forth, I march. Back and forth.

Sunshine sparkles through the windows, warming the air, and my office smells like rug-cleaner and fresh paper. This room is more familiar to me than any other in the world, and yet everything now seems off-kilter. Wrong.

Were the walls always that eggshell color?

Is that *really* my desk?

And my trusted assistant didn't really just quit... did she?

Because it doesn't add up. I pay Hazel stacks more than any other assistant in the city, and her benefits package is even better than mine. She gets everything, damn it, every possible perk that money can buy, and that's still not enough?

Growling, I rake both hands through my hair and tug. My headache squeezes my skull, and unease roils in my belly.

Because I *know* Hazel likes her work, and she loves her colleagues. She's always babbling on about them, telling me stories about this accountant who had a baby, that designer who's getting married, the janitor who's learning to knit. Every tedious detail. Hazel loves Grapevine.

She knows my employees better than I do. She wouldn't leave them without good reason.

There's something I'm not seeing here. Something must have chased her away. But what?

Striding to my desk, I snatch the phone from its cradle—and freeze. Because this is where habit tells me to bark at my assistant, yelling at her to get in here and fix the problem. This is where Hazel bounces in with her swishy blonde ponytail and her big doe eyes, practically fizzing with excitement at being

131

given a task.

Christ, it's like she was raised by golden retrievers. *No one* can be that perky—it's not natural. And yet... she is.

But perky or not, this isn't something Hazel can fix for me. Hazel *is* the damn problem.

She can't leave me.

This cannot happen.

When I throw myself back into my desk chair, it's because my legs won't hold my weight any longer. My muscles have stopped working, and my chest is icing over from the inside, and god, what is happening to me? What the hell is this nightmare? Why do my insides feel all wrong?

I'll double her pay.

Triple it.

I'll—Hazel can have this office, and I'll take her desk out there. Anything if it means keeping her close. My hand shakes as I press the intercom button, summoning her back, but there's no response. No creaking floor out there, no crackle of her sweet voice down the phone. She's not there.

I bury my face in my shaking hands.

Of all the blows I could weather, of all the losses I could take, this is not one of them.

This. Cannot. Happen.

* * *

There are three important meetings scheduled for today, and I cancel all of them. I'd cancel the party too if Hazel hadn't worked so hard on it for months, but I won't do that to her. Besides, it will only hurt my cause.

There's a private bathroom attached to my office, and I lock myself in there for the next hour, drowning myself under a long, hot shower. The steam fills my straining lungs and the heat soothes my taut muscles, but nothing seems to touch the ice spreading through my chest. It's a lost cause. *I'm* a lost cause.

I towel dry, thinking of Hazel.

Get dressed, thinking of Hazel.

Push back my damp hair and stare dead-eyed at the foggy mirror, searching for something, *anything*, that might tempt a woman like her to stay.

Stay—as my assistant, obviously. Nothing more. I won't kid myself that a pure ray of sunshine like Hazel would ever want... *that*... from a moody asshole like me.

Because what do I even have to offer her? Muscles and money and a special signed agreement with HR? That won't work. Hazel is a commitment type of girl. A *relationship* girl, and that is something I am ill-equipped for.

Doesn't matter. I'm getting off topic.

By the time I emerge in a cloud of soap-scented steam, Hazel's muffled voice floats through my office door once again. My numb legs carry me across the room, through the doorway to the antechamber and over to her desk, where I stand and loom over her, arms folded. My icy heart slams against my ribs.

"One second," Hazel says, covering the mouthpiece of her phone. She peers up at me, eyebrows pinching together. "Hey, boss. Is your hair wet?"

Yes. So?

I needed a scalding hot shower to reanimate my corpse. It happens.

"We're going out this afternoon." Away from these weird eggshell walls, closing in on me. Away from the empty,

133

pointless future looming ahead, barren of all joy and flapjack crumbs. "Wrap up whatever you need to finish here."

Hazel gapes. "But the party—"

"We'll get there in time for the set up. What's your address? Get someone to deliver your dress and whatever else you need to my apartment. You can get ready there."

"But I—"

"This is time sensitive, Hazel." Her notice period is two weeks, after all. Only two weeks. And in the meantime, I can't let her out of my sight—not if I want to be able to breathe. "If you want a good reference from me, I still expect your best work while you're here. That includes this afternoon."

An angry flush creeps up my assistant's throat, but she forces a smile onto her face. How many times has she done that for me before? Pretended everything is fine? Shit. Why didn't I pay attention? If I'd known she was unhappy, I could have fixed this mess long ago.

A tinny voice echoes down the phone, and Hazel jumps. "I'll be ready," she tells me, then turns back to her phone call. "Oh, I know! Aren't suppliers the worst?"

That's my cue to leave her be, to let her wrap up in her own time, but I don't move an inch. Don't think I can willingly leave Hazel's side until she agrees to stay. My body won't allow it.

When it's clear I'm not leaving, Hazel rolls her eyes and wraps up the call. The phone clicks back into its cradle, then she sighs up at me. Shrugs.

"I'm done here. Where are we going?"

"It's a surprise."

To both of us. Haven't thought that far ahead yet.

All I know is: I need Hazel by my side to feel okay.

Hazel

Leo Corbin has never taken me out on errands before. He's not the type to want company, you know? Too surly. He's more of a big, cranky storm cloud that drifts down the street, with people leaping to get out of his way. At least, that's how *I* think of him.

So it's weird seeing other people react to my boss, especially out here in the real world. After four years at Grapevine, bringing him coffees and soothing his prickly temper, I'm so used to seeing him through his employees' eyes.

The stern, brooding boss. Handsome but icy. *Unapproachable*.

Turns out there's another way to see him.

Because out here on the bright, sunshine-drenched sidewalk, Leo can't walk ten meters without someone batting their eyelashes at him, smiling a come-hither smile, or shamelessly raking him with their gaze. Even dogs strain on their leashes, trying to get closer to the giant, dark-haired man with a permanent scowl.

135

At his side, I am invisible. Hurrying to keep up with his long strides, and trying desperately to ignore the prickles of jealousy every time someone checks my boss out. Even the dogs.

And I get it, okay? Leo is gorgeous. A stone-cold ten. He's tall, broad-shouldered, and severe in that way that gives me full-body shivers, so I can't judge. I'm a card-carrying member of the Leo Corbin Simp Society—and yet if one more random pedestrian bites their lower lip at my boss, I am going to vomit on his pristine white shirt.

"Ugh." Call me petty, but after the most shameless eye-fucking yet, I can't help scoffing. "That redhead practically drooled on her shoes."

"Mm?" Leo glances down at me, distracted. "What are you talking about?"

"Her." My thumb jabs over my shoulder. Leo frowns behind us, nonplussed, then takes my elbow to guide me around a crack in the sidewalk. His hand print tingles against my bare arm. "That woman wanted to climb you like a tree, boss."

He harrumphs, turning his back on her. "I'm not open for climbing."

That should *not* make me so warm and gooey.

It's a beautiful day for heartbreak. The sidewalks bustle with people, and the golden sun warms the tops of our heads. The air is fresh, green leaves whisper on the trees that line this street, and after a while the rumble of distant traffic vibrates into my stiff muscles and soothes their knots. My chest loosens, and I breathe deeply.

I can do this.

I can let this man go.

I can walk away from the only all-consuming crush I've ever had; the only case of deep, unrequited love in my adult life. I've got this!

It's good that I'm leaving. There's no need to feel so hollow, like someone's scraped out my insides with a rusty spoon. There's no need to steal glances at my silent, solemn boss, fretting over whether he's taking the news well. Of course he's okay! Why wouldn't he be?

This is the right thing to do.

This is healthy. Smart.

So why do tears burn in the back of my eyes whenever I think about leaving Leo? Why does picturing another assistant behind my desk make me feel sick? Why does the thought of serving another boss, day in and day out, make me want to veer off this sidewalk into traffic?

"Hay fever?" my boss clips out, frowning straight ahead.

"Yeah," I lie, sniffling and dabbing my eyes with my wrist. "It's, um. It's all this pollen."

Leo sighs and takes my elbow again, tugging me into a small, cool store. "If I'd known, I'd have picked somewhere else," he says. "Tell me if you need to leave." It takes three long seconds of blinking around us before I realize what he's talking about.

Because: flowers.

Tubs and tubs of flowers, all freshly cut and fragrant. This whole store is an explosion of color, with delicate petals, green leaves, and the scent of damp soil. My heart climbs into my throat as I peer around us, struck dumb by this magical cave.

It's so beautiful in here, and I *love* flowers. What kind of monster doesn't?

But what on earth is Leo Corbin, hater of all gifts, doing in a florist's shop? And why am *I* here, called out on this urgent errand?

Ooooh no.

137

My stomach twists. There is one obvious reason.

A woman in a sky-blue apron bustles out of a backroom before I can ask, wiping her hands on a dishtowel. She's in her forties, with a kind mouth and generous curves, and black hair scraped back into a low bun.

Her gaze sweeps over Leo first, then me, and her eyes crinkle with pleasure.

"Oh, I love appointments like these," the florist says, striding forward. Her name badge says '*Hi! I'm Renata.*' "Half the time, these men don't care a fig what their girlfriend's favorite flower is. They just want me to pick so they get the brownie points, as though I can guess from nothing! But bringing you here— that's much better." She winks at me, and heat floods my cheeks. "You've got a good one here. Make sure you hang onto him."

"Oh... no..."

This is so embarrassing.

"The full experience, please," Leo says, flashing a dark card before placing it on the sales counter. His cheeks are as pale as ever, with no hint of a blush, so I guess this isn't awkward as hell for *him*. Must be nice.

"Is this for the party tonight?" I whisper as Renata marches to a display of roses, humming over the thorny stems. They rustle in the bucket as she picks out the prime flowers. "Because I planned decorations. It's all taken care of, I swear."

But hopefully that's it. Hopefully this man is not about to trample on my heart like a big, clumsy carthorse.

Leo fiddles with his shirt cuff. "No, it's not that."

"Then why—?"

Pale blue eyes turn on me, rooting me to the spot. "Can't a man buy flowers?"

"But—"

"I can," he interrupts, dark eyebrows spearing down. "I can buy whatever the hell I like. And for the next two weeks, you still work for me, Hazel. Correct? You'll still do what I say. And the task I want you to complete is to pick out your favorite flowers."

My hands ball into fists. This jerk! I swear to god.

"I'm waiting," Leo says.

Waiting. Scowling. Planting his feet and folding his arms, like he's ready to wait me out for hours if necessary. Like months could pass and the seasons could change outside this store, and he'd still be here, glaring down at me. Ugh.

Fine. Fine! I whirl around and stare blindly at a bucket of tulips.

"It would help if I knew what your woman is like so I can pick." Renata makes a small noise of dismay, but I can't look in her direction. Can't stand to see the disappointment—or worse, pity—in her eyes. "Or Renata could tell you. She has more experience with this than I do."

There's a long pause. Leo coughs once, then steps closer to my back. "Hazel... the flowers are for you."

Sunshine spreads through my veins, even as my brain throbs with confusion.

"So they're a goodbye gift?"

When I turn back, Leo is scowling at a tub of yellow dahlias, his stern mouth twisted in distaste. He straightens when I look at him, and then we're staring at each other. Lost.

The air changes. Gets thicker.

My hairline tingles.

But I won't overthink this. So many times over the last few years, I've kidded myself that the boss and I have shared these *moments.* Invisible sparks crackling between our fingertips when our hands accidentally brushed; a swooping feeling whenever we're alone in the elevator, like we're dropping down, down, down to the earth's core. All those times our eyes locked and it felt like time stood still.

I've told myself so many pretty stories; replayed those moments over and over in my head, until I lost track of what was a daydream and what was real.

"It's not goodbye." Leo speaks first, throwing down the words like a challenge. His chest puffs up, like we're fighters squaring up in the ring. "Because you're not leaving."

Ha. "You can tell yourself that if you like. And while you're at it, you can order the world to stop turning. I'll still be gone in two weeks."

Leo scowls at me, and for once in my life, I scowl back. The expression feels weird on my face, because I'm always the perky one. The happy-go-lucky girl next door. The ball of sunshine who cheers everybody else up, and makes sure people are happy and comfortable.

Not right now. Right now, my forehead is creased, and my eyes burn with frustration, and my cheeks are red-hot. I'm a first-time glarer, but I'm giving it my all.

"Pick your favorites," Leo mutters at last, turning away. "We're not leaving until you do." Then my boss stomps back outside, the door slamming shut behind him, and stands guard at the window, his back to the glass.

Silence stretches for the space of three heartbeats, before Renata sniffs and shakes herself.

"Well," the florist says. "Men, eh? Can't live with them, but can't get rid of them either. It's the basis of my whole business."

That's what I'm afraid of.

Leo

❦

Hazel chooses a simple bouquet of white daisies from the florist, then a small box of toffee-nut cookies from the bakery next door. After those two modest gifts, she point blank refuses to accept another thing from me, and insists on heading to the rooftop to help set up tonight's party.

Whatever. I don't care.

There never were any *errands.* I had no plans except spoiling her all day. Nothing else matters except keeping my assistant within arm's reach, and changing her mind about quitting—and sure, I'd rather do that while buying her a diamond necklace or hand-feeding her chocolate dipped strawberries, but we can lug around sun loungers on my building's rooftop if Hazel prefers.

After an hour of fussing with the furniture, she props her hands on her hips, breathing hard. Long flyaway hairs have frizzed out of her blonde ponytail, and her skin is dewy with sweat where it's not covered by her purple dress. All around us,

141

sun loungers have been dragged into clusters of two or three, safely away from the swimming pool's edge.

Static crackles across the rooftop as the band sets up their sound system over on the pop-up stage. It's a hot, sticky day, and we're on top of a skyscraper, held up to the sun's fiercest rays. Is Hazel drinking enough water? Does she need sunscreen?

"Should we fence it off somehow?"

Dabbing her wrist against her forehead, Hazel squints at the pool, with its sparkling turquoise water lapping the tiles. It would be so good to slip into that cool water right now. To soothe my heated skin, and feel the anguished pounding of my heart vibrate the water, and burn off this turmoil with fifty hard laps, barely coming up for air. Especially if Hazel came in with me.

Imagine it. That blonde ponytail trailing across the surface; those slippery wet legs twining around my waist...

"What if someone falls in?" she says.

"That's called natural selection."

"Leo!"

For god's sake. "Would you fence off a fountain?" I point out. "Or a lakeside?"

"Well, no. But—"

"There are no children invited tonight. No high risk guests. And let's say you roped the pool off—a rope wouldn't stop anyone falling in, would it?"

"I guess..."

She's still stewing, her big eyes fraught. That worried pinch between her eyebrows won't go away. My thumb itches to smooth it, then trace the length of her pert nose. Since when am I so desperate to touch her?

"I could hire a lifeguard," I hear myself offer. "Someone to blend in and hang around the sun loungers. There's still time."

Hazel beams up at me like I'm her hero. And fuck, *this* is the gift that finally warms her up to me? Not the flowers or the cookies. This is the trick to punching down the wall she's built between us?

A rent-by-the-hour lifeguard. This woman makes no sense. "It's done."

My footsteps echo against the rooftop tiles, and I tug my phone out of my pocket, weirdly shaken by that whole interaction. By that *smile*.

Because what if I'm going about this all wrong? What if there's something else Hazel wants from me that I'm not giving? Planting myself in a patch of shade, I close my eyes and let the breeze wash over my cheeks. My frozen heart is still numb inside me, the ice creeping through my chest.

One painful beat rattles my ribs. Two. Three.

Then I snap back into action and start typing on my phone, finding a last minute lifeguard. There's still time to figure Hazel out. Still time to fix this.

There has to be.

* * *

"What do you want from me, exactly?"

The question makes Hazel jump where she's loading up a refrigerator behind one of the pop-up bars. Crates of beer and wine bottles rest on the bar top, and Hazel lines their labels up neatly as she fills the chilled shelves. "What do you mean?" she asks, ducking her head. Her ponytail swishes over one shoulder.

143

Isn't it obvious? So far, guess work has gotten me nowhere. That means I need to go on the attack. After all, I didn't build a thriving business by being timid.

The sky all around us is stained pink, and the puffs of cloud are lit golden by the sunset. We've been working at this for hours already, stopping only for a rushed late lunch of deli sandwiches. The guests will arrive soon, and I'll grit my teeth and smile through the whole night, and then Hazel can finally forget about this nonsense and focus on what is important: staying with me.

"You need to tell me how I can stop you from quitting."

"I already have quit," Hazel points out, lining up another beer bottle with a soft clink. "It's done." And she doesn't need to set up these bars, doesn't need to help with every single task, but my assistant actually *likes* being helpful. She told me once that it soothes her nerves.

Do her nerves need soothing right now?

Well, they can join the damn club.

"There must be something." Rounding the bar to start loading a second refrigerator, I steal measuring glances at Hazel as she works. She *seems* fine. A little flushed, maybe, but then we've been in the sun all afternoon, and I'm keeping an eye on that. Already made her sip her way through two big water bottles. Already made her apply sunscreen as I stood over her, glowering whenever she missed a spot. "You liked the lifeguard thing."

Hazel hums, lifting a Pinot Grigio from the crate and scanning the label. "You've got me there, boss. I do like it when people don't drown."

She's missing the point.

"You liked that more than the flowers, I mean. And you didn't want a raise."

I already tried that approach—plus more paid vacation, a fancier desk chair, and a membership at the fancy wellness spa three blocks from the office. All afternoon, I've been calling offers across the rooftop. Nothing. Not even a nibble.

My girl-scout of an assistant cannot be tempted.

Soon to be *ex*-assistant.

Shit.

My frozen chest feels like it might cave in, but I wrestle the panic back down. That won't help. Nothing will help until I've solved this problem.

"It's a simple enough request." My tone is too harsh, my words too clipped, and I should handle this better but I can't. Not when she's threatening to suck all the meaning from my life. "Just tell me what you want from me, damn it."

Because if Hazel's not behind that desk, what's the point of going to the office at all? If I'm not working to give her the best possible salary and package, what's the point of Grapevine? What's the point of *me*?

If Hazel is not near, will my heart even fucking beat?

"There's nothing I want from you," Hazel says, mechanically filling the refrigerator shelves, but the back of my neck prickles. Something about the measured tone of her voice gives her away: she's lying! The beautiful wretch.

"Anything," I say, squaring up to her in the narrow bar space. "Anything at all. Name it and it's yours."

Hazel's lips press together in a thin line. And she keeps working, keeps lining up booze bottles like it's the most important task on earth, but I catch her elbow the next time she straightens up and hold her in place.

"Tell me."

String lights wink from the temporary roof above us. This whole rooftop has been transformed into a sea of twinkling lights, and they sparkle in my assistant's honey-brown eyes.

She juts her chin. "No. I mean—I can't. There's nothing."

"Tell me," I say again, squeezing her arm softly. Her bare skin is warm and soft beneath my palm, and the way my body reacts to the contact, you'd think I'd stripped Hazel bare and spread her beneath me.

My gut clenches.

My pulse throbs in my throat.

My temperature climbs and my throat bobs, swallowing nothing.

Want her. *Need her.*

"I don't... I mean, there's not..."

My assistant trails off, her chest rising and falling beneath that purple dress. We're closer, somehow. Gravitating nearer. My hand is on her bare arm, and her flyaway hairs dance on the breeze, and those soulful eyes flick down to my mouth and stay there.

Slam. Slam. Slam.

If my heart beats any harder, it'll punch clean through my rib cage.

Hazel is still looking at my mouth.

Is that—does she want—?

"What if I kissed you?" My voice is hoarse, but I make the offer. Need to know. "What then? Would you stay?"

All the other sounds of the rooftop—the clatter and calls of the catering staff, the slosh of the pool, the flap of gazebos in the breeze—it all fades away to nothing.

Hazel's gaze shoots up to mine. Her pupils are blown.

And my common sense screams in the back of my head,

begging me to think this through, but I smother that voice with an imaginary pillow. Not now, damn it.

Body thrumming, I close the distance between us. Her dress brushes against my shirt, and Hazel lets out a soft whimper.

This can't be real.

But when I bend my head, going slow, she doesn't back away. No: Hazel pushes onto her toes and flings both arms around my neck, like she's been longing for this for years. Like it's been exhausting her tiny frame, trying to hold all this passion back.

Her mouth finds mine. Our lips brush, and our breath mingles in the twilight, and it's like a punch in the gut.

Need curls through me, buckling my knees and stealing my air. Don't care if swarms of hired staff can see us here; don't care if they gossip. Don't care about anything except the maddening woman in my arms.

Cupping the sides of Hazel's throat, I slant our heads and kiss her again, harder. *Harder.* Long and deep and desperate, tongues sliding, teeth nipping, and I've never felt anything like this before in my whole lonely life.

She's just so fucking *sweet.* Warm and perfect, like a mug of hot cocoa, with her needy whimpers and her clinging arms and the way she arches against me, silently begging for more. It's so much more than I bargained for and so much less than I need, and I've lost track of the sky above and the ground below. Lost track of everything except Hazel's lips on mine.

What was the plan here, again? How will this work?

"*Mmph.*" She gives as good as she gets, kissing me eagerly. As though I'm a man she could truly desire; as if this is shaking her world apart too. But that can't be right, because of all people, Hazel knows what I'm truly like.

The moods. The surliness.

The way I'm incapable of love. After all, my parents hated each other and me. I never learned the right way to do any of this nonsense.

And sure, I *want* Hazel. That's been clear from the moment I met her four years ago, when the sun rose in my gloomy universe. And yes, my body craves hers in a way that I've never wanted anyone else, but it's deeper than that—like she settles my soul, or something.

But that's impossible.

And this is only one kiss—to make her stay.

One kiss.

God.

Tearing my mouth away feels wrong. *Wrong.* It's all wrong to take my hands away and step back; all wrong to feel cool dusk air wash over my front. Everything about this is wrong, and nothing is right in the world unless our hands are on each other.

"We should get ready for the party," I mutter.

A few minutes alone will give me a chance to scrape up my last surviving brain cells.

"S-sure. Okay." Cheeks pink, Hazel wobbles out of the pop-up bar. She doesn't look back at me.

Hazel

❧❧❧

My boss makes zero sense. One minute, he's gazing at me hungrily, yanking me to his front, and kissing me until my head spins. Making all my heartsick daydreams of the last four years, all those imaginary kisses that played like a movie reel in my head, pale in comparison to the real thing. Drowning me in perfect, overwhelming details.

Like his heat.

His *hunger*.

The hard planes of his chest and the little growls in the back of his throat, and the way he kissed along my jaw, breathing in the scent of my skin like he wanted me to fill his lungs.

Then... this. We're back to cold, professional distance between us again, like nothing ever happened. Like it meant nothing. If I didn't know better, I'd think I hallucinated the whole freaking thing—except my lips are kiss-swollen, and there's a telltale slickness between my legs that will not stop tormenting me as I walk. Thoughts blurry, I dodge a server carrying a stack of trays and stumble across the rooftop. The band is warming up, random notes humming on the breeze.

Gotta get inside.

Gotta change for tonight.

And hell, I'm going to need a long, cold shower first to get my head on straight; to calm the ache in my lower belly and my feverish pulse and all the silly, foolish voices whispering in my head that *he wants me, he wants me, Leo actually wants me.*

Leo Corbin does not want me.

Leo Corbin does not do relationships. Period.

And if he ever broke that rule, it would never be for me. I annoy him too much, driving him to distraction with my perkiness first thing in the morning. He's grumbled about how unbearable I am more times than I could ever count—and I try really, really hard not to count.

But... unbearable, am I?

That kiss didn't *feel* like he found me unbearable. Not for those few perfect minutes, at least. No: it felt like Leo Corbin was ready to sling me over his shoulder and carry me across the city rooftops, King Kong style.

Back inside the building, my spare key lets me into the boss's penthouse apartment. I've been here dozens of times before, running errands for Leo, but my heart has never raced like this as I step inside. My skin has never flushed hot, like I'm doing something wrong.

I'm not.

I'm *not.*

Leo is the one who told me to get ready here, and I remind myself of that fact over and over as I gobble down two of my toffee-nut cookies in the kitchen in place of dinner, shower in his bathroom, dress in his bedroom, and keep my gaze fixed on anything except the bed. Still, it's impossible to miss the faint spicy scent of his aftershave. What color are Leo's bed sheets?

No! I will not look.

If I do, I'll probably rope myself to the headboard and beg my boss to ravish me just once for old times' sake. Sane, normal assistants don't do that.

So, nope. Not crossing any lines in here, thank you, brain. Instead I tiptoe back to the safety of the living area and slide on my strappy high heels with a wince.

Ouch. I stand up straight and shake out my arms. My feet throb like crazy, and it's already been a long day, but I'm sure that my silvery heels and pink cocktail dress do nothing to hide that fact. At least I've redone my ponytail, smoothing down those stray, frizzy hairs, and dabbed some gloss on my lips.

The key sliding into the lock gives me barely any warning. The door swings open, and Leo strides inside, barreling into the kitchen.

He's still in his work clothes from earlier, the white shirt open at the collar and rumpled by our kiss—and duh, of course he hasn't changed yet. I've been hogging his apartment.

Leo's black hair is wind-ruffled, and dark shadows cling beneath his icy blue eyes. He looks wan as he chugs a glass of water; today is taking a toll on him too.

Is he okay?

Wish I could cancel this party. Even though it's selfish, even though I've put in months and months of stressful work, I'd love nothing more right now than to close that door and block out the rest of the world. To hole up in this penthouse with the boss and let him persuade me again to stay with a kiss; to switch on his fancy remote-control fireplace and curl up together on the sofa for more... negotiations.

Because Leo kissed me.

He *kissed* me.

Doesn't make any sense.

But my stupid heart doesn't care about logic and boring stuff like that—it's too busy doing cartwheels around my chest.

"You look…" Leo trails off with a frown, placing his empty glass down with a thud.

My excitable heart sinks, finally simmering down, and I pluck at the pink fabric. It *seemed* fine when I checked myself in the bathroom mirror, but maybe this outfit is all wrong. "Oh. Okay. I could change back into the purple dress from earlier?"

"What?" Leo's frown deepens, then he jerks his head from side to side. "No! That's not what I—no. You look nice. That's what I was going to say."

"Nice," I mumble. "Thank you."

And I'm not digging for compliments, I swear, this man just scrambles my brain with a fork whenever he's near. But Leo huffs and folds his arms, leaning back against the counter like I'm being difficult.

"Beautiful. You look beautiful, Hazel. Alright? Is that what you wanted to hear?"

Um. No? No one wants compliments through gritted teeth.

"I'll head up to the roof," I say, all business. No point wallowing, is there? And arguing sure won't make things better. Besides, I'll be gone in two short weeks, and these tiny stabs of disappointment won't hurt me anymore. "You change and follow, then we can greet the guests as they arrive."

"Wait, Hazel."

"Mm?" Tugging my dress straight, I won't meet the boss's eye. Why should I? He kissed me, then bit my head off. Life is too damn short for this nonsense, and that is why I'm leaving.

"Will you stay?" Leo presses, gripping the counter hard, and it's so freaking rich of him to ask me that now, right after grumping at me over nothing.

"No."

The boss puffs up, outraged. "But I kissed you. We agreed—"

"*We* didn't agree on anything. You tried something and it didn't work. Nice attempt, though." My heels clack on the floor as I march past, and jeez, I hate playing hardball like this. Hate walking away when I can feel the misery pouring off him in waves, but what else can I do?

This man could crush my heart without a second thought— and he doesn't even want it. He wants me to stay as his assistant, nothing more, and he's willing to toy with my feelings to win his prize.

I should be madder than this. I should stomp and yell.

Instead, I'm just tired.

"Follow me up when you're ready."

* * *

For the next few hours, Leo Corbin is my handsome, brooding shadow.

He stands so close our arms brush as we greet the guests arriving on the rooftop; he fetches me drinks and canapes, fussing over whether I'm hydrated. When my shoe strap comes undone on the way to check on the band, it's Leo who kneels down and fixes it, those blunt fingertips brushing over my bare ankle and making me tingle.

Mind games.

That's what this is.

Just another ploy by my wily boss to make me want to stay

with him, fetching his coffees and scheduling his meetings for as long as we both shall live. Another attempt to wear me down, crumbling my will power with sweet gestures and rumbled kind words.

No! It cannot work.

I *can't* stay.

"Would you like to dance?" Leo asks as I hover at the edge of the dance floor, checking for dropped glasses or any other trip hazards. Nothing. The staff are doing a great job tonight, but I can't seem to unclench, no matter how reliable they are.

This party is my responsibility. And now it'll be the thing everyone here remembers me for—if they remember me at all.

A lump sticks in my throat. I blink up at Leo, confused. "What?"

"A dance." He takes my hand, his expression more patient than I have ever seen, and tows me gently into the crowd. "You've watched enough people having fun, Hazel. Now you should try it."

"But I... but we..." My legs are clumsy as I trip after the boss, and when he turns to face me, I practically fall against his chest. "Okay, fine."

Curious glances flick toward us from all directions—because Leo Corbin does not dance. He does not engage with mere mortals. And yet here he is, lifting my arms around his neck before placing his hands on my waist, the heat of them searing through the thin fabric of my dress. Here he is, turning us in steady circles as the band plays a smooth song, staring down at me with those frosty blue eyes.

Leo's mouth curves up on one side. Holy shit, is that a smile?

"You needn't look so terrified, Hazel. I won't step on your feet."

"Only metaphorically."

His laugh is rumbly and so nice.

"Stay," Leo murmurs, squeezing my waist with his big, gentle hands. "Stay with me."

"No."

Emotions war on his face, battling for dominance, and I watch them play across his features, fascinated.

I'm used to Bored Leo. Irritated Leo. Focused Leo. Hangry Leo.

Not Emotionally Tortured Leo.

"Tell me why," he demands.

My fingers scrunch against his lapels. "I can't."

"Can't stay? Or can't tell me why?"

"Both."

The boss puffs out a breath, but he doesn't scold me or storm off, even though this conversation must be maddening for him. Instead, he moves us closer, hands gripping possessively at my sides.

My tummy quivers.

My heartbeat pulses between my legs.

Thumbs trace along my sides, tickling me through my thin dress.

Stars wink overhead, and laughter and chatter buzz beneath the music. The rooftop is thronged with guests, everyone bright-eyed and excited to be here, on the mysterious boss's rooftop. Seeing his pool, eating his canapes, drinking from his open bars. Leo Corbin is secretly a generous man—people just don't notice that fact when he's glaring at them.

"Will you tell me before you leave?" Dread curls through the boss's low voice, his expression pained.

"Yes," I promise.

I can do that much. After everything Leo Corbin has given me, surely I owe him the truth.

One final confession, one rip of the band aid, and then we'll draw a line under this whole messy affair.

Leo

H azel stays on the rooftop until the last guest has been poured into the car service we've provided for tonight. She thanks the band personally and helps coil their cables. She helps the staff to pick up stray glasses and empty beer bottles, then fills crates with dirty dishware ready to go down to the catering van. Hell, she'd probably ride there tonight and single-handedly load all their dishwashers if she could.

"Oh no you don't." Snagging her wrist as Hazel moves to follow the last hired staff off the roof, I hold her back. "You're done for tonight, sweetheart. Take those shoes off."

She's been hobbling for the last hour when she thinks no one is watching. Well, joke's on Hazel, because I'm *always* watching, and she can't hide her aching feet from me.

My assistant rolls her eyes, but when I kneel and gesture for her foot, she leans on my shoulder and offers one leg.

Such graceful arched feet. Such feminine toes, the nails painted pink.

157

Christ. Am I suddenly a foot man? This woman has ruined me.

"You did way too much tonight." Scolding Hazel will make me feel better. Teasing the fiddly little straps undone, I slide off one high heel then the other, placing them carefully on the roof.

The stone is still warm, radiating the heat of the day, even as the wind whips across the empty rooftop and ruffles Hazel's dress and hair. Without the crowds and the gazebos to get in the way, the wind moans and pushes her tiny frame so hard she stumbles.

That's enough of that. Straightening up, I take Hazel's hand and tug her across the rooftop to the pool. Cool water will make those toes feel better—and if she sits, she'll be sheltered from the worst of the wind.

"Do you think everyone had a good time tonight?" Her voice is thin and tired, and she clings to my hand like a lifeline as I lead her to the pool. So goddamn sweet. Always worrying about other people, always thinking about her coworkers and friends, while Hazel has worked herself into the ground for this party.

"Yes. Sit on the edge and put your feet in the water."

A hiss escapes her as her feet break the surface, but once she's settled, Hazel tips her head back with a blissed-out sigh. "That's better."

"I'm very wise." Dragging a sun lounger closer, I sit down and stare at the back of my assistant's blonde head. Her long ponytail dangles between her shoulder blades, ruffled by the breeze. What I'd give to wrap that rope of hair around my fist...

"Modest, too."

When I crack a smile, my face aches from the unfamiliar motion. My insides are plummeting, falling into nothingness.

Would Hazel ever care for me too?

Could she ever... *love* me?

What if I worked every day to earn her love and loyalty? What if I turned all the fierce dedication and focus that I used to build Grapevine onto my assistant, building something new between us? Something real?

My frozen heart thumps harder, prickling back to life.

Yeah. I could do that.

I *want* to do that.

What else is life about if not Hazel? Why have I been so stubborn? So blind? Sure, I'm a clueless jackass when it comes to matters of the heart, but I've got a brain, haven't I? I can learn.

For her, I'll learn anything.

"Hazel," I say quietly. She hums, eyes still closed and face tilted to the stars. "Will you tell me now? Will you tell me why you won't stay?"

Just like that, the peace flees her expression. Her forehead pinches, and her shoulders go stiff, and Hazel's mouth presses together in a tight line. And I'm opening my mouth to coax her, to make those shoulders relax, when my assistant pushes off the side of the pool and plunges into the water fully dressed.

"Hazel!"

I lunge up, panic choking my throat. Shit! Can she swim? What if that dress tangles around her legs? What if she's too tired after a long day in the sun?

Doesn't matter. I'm already charging forward, diving in after her fully clothed. Already thrashing through the ghostly water, lights glowing from the sides of the pool, desperate to reach her.

A small body. Pink fabric twisting in the water. An elbow in my gut.

We break the surface, both gasping for breath.

"What—*Leo*—what the hell is wrong with you?" Hazel fights out of my arms and turns on me, soaked and furious. Her eye makeup has smudged, and her pink dress clings to every inch of her pint-sized body. "I'm not drowning, you ass."

My mouth opens and closes as I gape at her, enraged.

"You jumped in! Who does that? Of course I panicked!"

How am I the bad guy here? I just ruined a perfectly good tux to rescue my assistant and now I'm the villain. Make sense of that.

"Well, I can swim, thank you."

I will not splash her; will not dunk her beautiful head under. I am not five years old.

"Good to know. I'm glad this wasn't a *dangerously* insane thing to do, just unhinged. You know, if you're that afraid to answer my question, you can say so. There's no need to drown yourself to escape a simple, adult conversation—"

Water splashes over me in a small wave, and I wipe my eyes, spluttering. My assistant glares at me, furiously treading water. "Oh, shut up. It's not that easy and you know it."

I *know* it? What the hell do I know?

"You splashed me," I say like an idiot. Hazel huffs and does it again. "I—you—stop splashing me! Come here, you little witch."

With all the times I pictured myself wrestling with Hazel, this scenario never came up: both of us fully dressed in my private pool, our evening wear soaked to our skin, bickering and grappling as water sloshes over the sides. Overhead, a

160

cloud drifts across the moon like it's shielding it from our nonsense, but I've never felt so alive.

She's a wriggly little thing. All elbows and knees, with zero shame about trying to catch me in the junk. And I'd give her some space, would be more careful about crossing this line, except my assistant is giggling like a maniac, splashing and kicking and—Jesus—*biting*. Booming out a laugh, I wrestle her around until she's facing me, bare legs wrapped around my hips.

Hazel pokes out her tongue. My fingers flex on her waist.

It's inevitable, really.

We slam together like two wild beasts, kissing savagely, still half wrestling. And I'm bigger than her but she's nimble and slight, and more to the point, a single brush of her lips melts my brain. I'm helpless to do anything except stagger to the pool's edge, leaning back against the tiles while Hazel claws at me, kissing and nipping, yanking on my sodden clothes.

"You—are—such a jerk!"

I know.

I know I am, and she's an angel. She's *my* angel, and she's wet and warm and twined around me like ivy, kissing me like she never wants to stop. Neither do I.

"This," Hazel says, panting between kisses, "is why I can't stay. *This* is what I want, it's what I've wanted from you for years, and it's killing me. I need to leave. Can't you see that?"

My hands slide down to her ass and squeeze. So perfect. So sweet. "You're not going anywhere."

There's an enraged growl, then Hazel kisses me again, sucking hard on my bottom lip. And I thought I was already as hard as a man can get after all that wrestling, but hey, guess I'm wrong, because lust arrows through my gut and my cock stiffens so much it could drill through the pool wall.

"You don't want me!" she says against my lips.

Yanking her ass closer, I drag her over my hardness, riding her up and down my length. "You sure about that?"

Because of course I want her. Hazel is my lifeblood. She's the heart in my chest and the air I breathe. She's everything good and warm and right in the world, and maybe it took me a while to see, but I'm done being an idiot about this. Done fighting this.

And I am never, ever letting her go.

"You're staying," I tell her, trailing kisses down her neck and sucking a mark onto her delicate skin. She whimpers, clutching closer to my shoulders, her hips still riding my length of her own accord. "Not as my assistant, though I'd like that too. God knows my days are empty without you. No, Hazel. You're staying with *me*."

Her breath catches. "Leo."

"I was an idiot not to see it. An idiot to fight this thing. But I'm done screwing this up, and I'll spend the rest of our lives making this up to you, sweetheart. Convincing you to stay with me every single day."

Now I'm running out of words, running out of brain cells, but thankfully Hazel moans and kisses me again, hard. My heart flares hot, searing my insides, melting the last of the ice inside me, and thank god. Thank god.

A small hand travels down my front and tugs at my belt.

"Prove it," Hazel says. "Make me yours."

Hazel

⊰❦⊱

My boss lifts me out of the pool first, moonlight glinting in the shower of water droplets. The wind roams over my wet skin, goosebumps prickling from the cold, but I don't have time to shiver before Leo is here too, tugging me to the sun lounger then wrestling my soaked dress over my head.

"Damn thing," he mutters as he does it, black hair dripping in his eyes, and god, he's so beautiful under the stars. Like some ancient Roman god rather than my cranky boss in a sodden tux.

The dress lands with a splat.

Then I'm crowded back, guided down onto the lounger, and Leo strips off his own clothes before crawling on top of me, every movement ruthlessly efficient.

His body heat is delicious. So overwhelming and warm. Leo is the perfect muscly blanket to chase away the chill, and when he kisses me again, deep and soulful, I could burst with joy.

This is happening.

This is happening!

I've loved him for so long, *pined* for him for so long, and I never thought... never dreamed...

Hang on.

"Do you still find me annoying?" I ask as my boss peels down the left cup of my bra, sucking the hard bead of my nipple into his mouth. He grunts, tongue swirling, and that coil of heat travels all the way down my body to twist between my legs.

Leo pulls back long enough to nuzzle my small boob. "Obviously not. Wait, no—I never found you annoying. Why would you think that?"

He frowns at me, genuinely troubled, and I sputter out a laugh, weaving my fingers through his damp hair. "Because of all the things you said and did."

Another scowl—but this one comes with fiery heat in his eyes. "I'll show you what I think of you, Hazel."

And Leo kneels up and grabs two fistfuls of my blue lace panties. He tears them apart in one go, muscles shifting, like he's ripping wet tissue paper and not thick, soaked lace, then tosses both scraps over his shoulder into the darkness.

Leo pauses and raises an eyebrow at me. I gape.

"Underwear is expensive, you jerk!"

"I'll buy you new ones," is all Leo says, pushing my thighs apart. "A new pair every day if you let me tear them off you."

Oh god, I will, won't I? My body moves easily under his touch, legs flopping open, completely compliant, because I am a giant weenie who loves her boss's secret caveman side. He could touch me with a fingertip and I'd move. He could tear every scrap of clothing off me and I'd still assume the position: face down, ass up, quivering with eagerness.

Ah, well. Dignity is overrated.

When Leo's scowl zeroes in between my legs, fixing there, I bite down on my lip hard. Every self-conscious atom in my body screams at me to close my legs, to hide away from his inspection, but Leo's breathing gets heavier, his nostrils flare, and I don't want to shatter this moment.

Want to see what he'll do.

How he'll lay claim to me.

"This," Leo says at last, grating out the words. Fingertips coast along my slit, spreading my slickness and tickling me until I squirm. "This. This is mine. *You're* mine, Hazel."

"Okay."

My wobbly agreement brings out a shark's smile.

Then he's leaning down, shifting around, shouldering his way between my legs; pausing to kiss my hip, my stomach, my belly button, my thigh. Leo peppers my whole body with kisses, including my awkward angles and every dimpled, squishy bit, before his breath finally mists across my most sensitive area.

"You're so sweet, Hazel." Leo sounds dazed, staring between my legs, stroking and rubbing and watching me arch and gasp. "So perfectly sweet. Bet you taste it too. Like sugar on my tongue."

The flat of Leo's tongue strokes me from ass to clit. It's a thorough, shameless, *claiming* lick, and my head tips back on a gasp.

Holy. Shit.

Hot breaths puff against my inner thighs, and my boss is licking, sucking, nibbling, spreading me wider on this sun lounger and *devouring* me like I'm his own personal feast. And maybe I don't taste like literal sugar, but Leo Corbin does not seem to mind—not if those pleased, hungry grunts are anything to go by.

Wet heat swirls over my clit.

It all feels so freaking good my eyes cross.

And thank god this is a private rooftop, because if someone else came up here, if they found us like this... I'm not sure I could stop.

"Mine," Leo rumbles, his words vibrating against my clit. Another deep lick. "You're *mine*."

No arguments here.

I've been his for four years. All those coffees I brought, all those times I smiled at his cranky face as he stepped off the elevator, all those phone calls I fielded and appointments I booked...

I did it all with so much love.

"Hazel." The sun lounger rasps across the stone tiles as Leo forces us back an inch. My boss presses a very hot, very solid, very *real* kiss on my hip. "My perfect girl. Fuck, I need you. Need you right now. Roll over."

Giddy with desire, my limbs all loose and clumsy, I flop over and scramble to my hands and knees. *Yes.* Want this so badly.

"Next time, we'll do this in a bed." A strong hand smooths down my spine, making my tense muscles go all melty. Arching my back, I smile like a goofball at the silent, sparkling pool. He said 'next time', right? "It'll be romantic. I'll do this properly, Hazel, I swear, but right now..."

Leo's other hand twists my ponytail, wrapping it around his hand once, twice, three times. The sharp tug tilts my head back, scalp prickling, and molten heat swirls between my legs. I gasp up at the stars, so ready, so thrilled.

Oh god, I *need* him.

"Do it. Please, Leo, do it. Oh my gosh. Don't make me wait." I'm babbling, my mouth running ahead of my fevered brain, but I don't care. I'm happy to beg Leo Corbin if he'll give me what I need: if he'll take this maddening, tickly, *hollow* feeling away and stretch me full.

"Relax," he says, his tone so gentle even as he strokes my spine again, touch masterful and firm. "Let me in, sweetheart."

Something blunt notches at my entrance.

Wriggling my thighs wider, I force myself to breathe.

Leo

Hazel is trembling. Her muscles shudder under my palm as I stroke her back, and her thighs twitch as she spreads her legs wider. Steady breaths float up from the sun lounger—she's counting inhales and exhales—and I'd stop, I'd call this whole thing off, panicking that she's stressed, if she weren't so desperately slick and needy. The evidence glints in the starlight.

She *wants* this.

My perfect little assistant wants me as badly as I want her. Those hips tilt up for me, urging me to take her already, and when my shaft nudges against her entrance, she lets out a strangled moan.

"You're sure?"

Because I'd never hurt her. I'm going to love this woman until the day I die, and there's no rush; we don't need to do this tonight. I could dress Hazel again, take her inside, bundle her into a hot shower and order takeout to stop her stomach from rumbling. That works for me too. It would still be the best night of my life.

But: "*Please*," Hazel begs, ass wiggling from side to side, coaxing me on. Taunting me. "Please, Leo. I need you."

Ah, hell.

When I grab her peachy ass with one hand, when I press the first inch inside her, Hazel is tighter and hotter than I ever dreamed. She's a slick little furnace, strangling my shaft even as her body sucks it deeper, and the *noises* she makes, scrabbling at the sun lounger, testing my hold on her hair...

Jesus Christ.

Those breathy little moans will haunt me to my deathbed.

"M-more," Hazel says, fingertips digging into the lounger so hard they turn bloodless. "*More*, Leo."

Flexing my grip on her ponytail, I grit my teeth and press forward again.

Draw back slightly, then nudge inside.

Out, in.

Back, deeper.

She's *so* tight.

And I'd worry about that, worry that Hazel doesn't really want this, except she's moaning and whimpering like a champ, squirming on my cock, and she's so slick that I glide forward easily enough. Another reason for her tightness presents itself in my brain, the logical conclusion, and my newly awakened heart stutters in my chest.

"Have you done this before, sweetheart?"

I'm half hope, half dread. It would be such a gift, and such a responsibility.

"N-no," Hazel says, throwing her hips back to take another inch of me inside. "But I know I want this. Please."

Her trust spreads through me, sparkling like sunshine.

And—as if I could fucking stop. A helicopter could appear above this rooftop, a whole SWAT team could parachute down, guns drawn and blazing, and I'd be helpless to do anything except keep thrusting, pulling her hair, squeezing her ass. Working my assistant into a quivering puddle.

Only Hazel could stop me now, and she's too busy groaning with pleasure, rocking back on my length. Pulling firmly on her ponytail, I arch her back even further, drawing her like a bow. Drops of water from the pool gleam on her back, tinted silver in the darkness.

"You're perfect." The words grit out of me, and I find a rhythm now, thrusting into my assistant from behind. The sun lounger creaks beneath us, and the wind whips across the rooftop, but there's no one to witness this but the stars. "You're so fucking perfect, Hazel. Look at you, taking my cock. You were built for this. Built for me."

Hazel spasms around my length, getting impossibly slicker.

"Leo," she sighs. "Leo."

Teeth gritted, blood boiling, I reach around and rub her clit. Hazel bucks and moans, so wild and free, and I plant a foot on the rooftop to keep from toppling off the damn sun lounger.

She won't shake me that easily. Not until she comes for me, pretty and flushed, and shows me all the noises she can make.

It doesn't take long. A few deep thrusts, hips angled to hit all the sensitive spots inside her, with a few firm circles of her clit. Just like that, Hazel throws back her head and cries out, loud and fractured, as her channel clamps down, fluttering around my cock.

The *heat* of her. Jesus Christ.

I come so hard it's almost painful. Fill her up, painting her insides with spurt after hot spurt, cramming her body full of my seed, and it's so darkly satisfying, staking this claim. Who knew I'd be such a caveman with my girl?

"Oh," Hazel says, collapsing forward on wobbly arms. I stay inside her, throbbing. "Oh my *god*."

Yeah.

That was—something else.

How long until we can go again?

* * *

Two years later

I'd be lying if I said I didn't like the sight of Hazel under my desk, but today, it's not quite right.

We've done this a hundred times before. My perky, always helpful wife simply *loves* abandoning her own desk to crawl under mine and help me relax, and who am I to stop her? Only the luckiest bastard on earth, that's who. I know a small miracle when I see it, and I have never, ever stopped my wife from going under there before. I'm not crazy.

But it's different now that she's pregnant. Hazel's not too far along; her bump is barely visible, but she's already moving a little awkwardly, and shit, what if her back aches while she's down there? What if her knees hurt? What if—

"Up." Throwing my chair back, I scoop my wife beneath her armpits and lift her out from under my desk. "Up you come. You're not going under there today."

Hazel huffs, smacking at my hands, but she lets me sit her on top of my desk without too much of a fight. She folds her arms and hits me with a glare.

"Just because I'm pregnant doesn't mean that I'm helpless,

171

Leo."

"I know that."

Obviously. But if Hazel thinks I'm going to let my pregnant wife crawl on the ground for me, she is so incredibly wrong. That game is fun—usually.

But I'm not in the mood to watch Hazel crawl these days. I'm in the mood to spread my wife's legs and worship her as she deserves.

"Look at that frown." I tut, nudging her knees apart, and Hazel grumps but allows it. There's a flash of pink lace as her legs widen. "I thought *I* was the cranky one."

And yet here I am, smiling so hard my cheeks ache, and there's my usually-bubbly wife—pouting because I won't let her get sore knees. It's a topsy-turvy day, but I love it.

This feels right.

Everything feels right with Hazel.

Sliding that ring on her finger; choosing a new home to start a family; coming to work together every day. All perfect. Even the small, mundane stuff like grocery shopping and arguing over which movie to watch—it all feels good with Hazel. Whenever I'm with her, I have this bone-deep certainty that I'm in the right place at the right time.

"You'll have a new assistant soon." Those arms tighten over Hazel's chest, and her lips tighten. "You'll be here with her, and I'll be…"

Lunging forward, I catch my wife with a deep, searing kiss, my heart thundering against my ribs. She kisses me back just as desperately, clinging to my shoulders, as I reach beneath her skirt and pull her panties aside.

"You're jealous," I pant, tearing my mouth away and pressing a finger inside her. Hazel arches and groans, already so wet

172

for me. "You're actually jealous. That's most ridiculous thing I've ever heard. Hazel, I don't *see* other women. Not like that. Honestly, I never did. I only see you, I fucking orbit around you, and every day that we're apart I'll be counting down the minutes until I'm home with you again."

She flings her arms around my neck, riding my hand. I've got two fingers inside her now, and she's so ready. So eager. "Really? You promise?"

How can she not *know*?

"You'll pick my assistant." Trailing kisses down her throat, I suck a bruise onto her skin, because Hazel's not the only territorial one here. Every time another man so much as looks at her, I growl, so I understand. "Pick an old grandmother. Pick a man. I don't care, not for a goddamn second, and if it makes you feel better—"

"It… it does. I mean, I *do* trust you." Hazel gasps as I shove my hips between her thighs, fumbling at my belt. She tugs on my waist, urging me closer. "I do trust you, Leo, I swear. It's just all these crazy hormones… this pregnancy brain…"

"It's done." Problem solved, and I don't care if it's a reasonable demand or not. My wife can demand the moon on a platter. "You'll pick my assistant, and you'll burst in here whenever you like, and I'll rush home to you at the end of the day. And I'll *show* you how ridiculous it is for you to worry. How gone I am for you."

We crash together in a blur of half-shed clothes and fevered kisses. The curve of Hazel's stomach presses against my front, and my heart pangs in my chest.

She *is* mine. Hazel's mine, and I'm hers, and this baby will swell our family to three members. I can't wait.

"Let me show you what you do to me," I say, notching at her

entrance. "Let me prove it."

And my perfect wife takes me inside with a sigh.

* * *

Thanks for reading the Night to Remember series! I hope you loved it. :)

For more HEAs at the office, check out the Grumps Unleashed series, starting with Grump Gone Wild. *I'm fake-dating the man of my dreams. But these feelings? They're all too real.*

And for a bonus instalove story, grab your copy of Something Sweet. *I spend every Valentine's Day baking cookies for my friends and neighbors. But the bad boy who just moved to town? He's hungry for something else...*

Happy reading!

xxx

Teaser: Grump Gone Wild

My boss pops the question on a rainy Thursday after lunch.

Not *the* question, obviously. That would be too perfect, too dreamlike—and pretty weird, since for all the years I've worked for him, despite my ginormous crush, Sebastian Bamford has only ever seen me as his zany assistant.

No, the beautiful genius summons me into his top floor office with a few curt words through the intercom, then waits behind his huge desk, jaw clenched.

"Felicity."

Despite my nudging, he's only ever called me Fliss twice in our whole acquaintance. Once at the company holiday party two years ago, when he greeted me solemnly by the pop up bar. I remember it vividly, not just because of the name thing, but because he wore a black knitted sweater instead of his usual suit, and his cheeks were pink from walking down the frosty street. *Swoon.*

The second time was when I had three days off work with a stomach flu. Sebastian called me at home on the third day, to 'check whether I needed anything'. Really, I think he suspected I was playing hooky.

Um, as if.

Not because I care so much about emails and appointments and refilling the water cooler cups, to be clear. But to willingly lose a day with Sebastian Bamford? The sexy, bossy nerd of my dreams? Are you crazy?

"I have a strange request." He's staring out of the huge windows. Raindrops patter against the glass, then streak down and blur the city skyline. Downtown looks like one giant smudge.

"Okay. What is it, sir?"

His mouth flattens, and he keeps scowling outside. I wait, shifting from foot to foot, but... nothing.

Alrighty.

I'm used to my boss's moods, so I distract myself with mental notes. Like: that potted plant in the corner needs water. And Sebastian has that video conference at two, the one with the German team. Should I double-check the translator? Wait, I did that already. But should I triple-check?

"It's not work-related," he says.

I bite the inside of my cheek, suddenly laser-focused. The air hums through the AC. "I'm very discreet, sir. You can trust me."

Trust me... Confide in me... Maybe love me back one day... Are you listening, universe? Just putting it out there.

"It's delicate," Sebastian says.

He's killing me here. "I'm sure I can handle it."

Because seriously, whatever it is, I've got this. Picking up his dry cleaning? Booking a doctor's appointment? Lying to his awful family for him? I'm there, no sweat, because I've been gone for my boss since day one. G-O-N-E. Head over heels for this beautiful grump, with his neat bronze hair and his tortoiseshell glasses and his perfectly pressed suits. I love him so much, it gives me indigestion.

When he rumbles orders at me in that deep voice—it's like he's reading me a sonnet. When he ignores me in the elevator, I swoon.

Gray eyes find mine, and shivers race down my spine. My face heats, despite the cool air flowing through a vent on the wall. This building should have a warning right above the entrance—*Caution: Boss may cause dizziness.*

"I have no right to ask you this, Felicity." He's so solemn; so pained. The rain-dulled daylight barely reaches his desk, and he's lit by the golden glow of a table lamp. "If you say no, it won't affect your work at all. Is that understood?"

Color me intrigued… though for the record, I'd do virtually anything for this man, including commit petty crimes. For Sebastian Bamford, my morals are scanty as hell.

He's just so *noble*. And hardworking and stern and delicious. Every second I'm near him, my fingers itch to yank on his tie. I want to climb into his lap and kiss him so hard I knock his glasses askew.

"Understood. What is it, sir?"

A muscle leaps in his jaw. Sebastian frowns over my shoulder into space, and the lamplight glints against his bronze hair. "I have a family event next weekend," he says slowly. "An important one, and… I need a date."

Oh my god. Oh my god.

Eeee!

I'm beaming wide, already floating up near the ceiling when he adds: "I'd like you to pretend to be my girlfriend. It would be fake, obviously. You'd get overtime."

I crash back down to the floor.

Overtime? He wants to pay me for this?

...*Fake*?

"It's purely business," Sebastian says, still frowning over my shoulder. When he finally looks at me, concern darts through his gray eyes. Guess my dismay is splashed all over my face. "I can hire someone else," he adds quickly. "I don't want to make you uncomfortable, Felicity. But I have neither the time nor the inclination to find a real date, and... well, you know my family."

After our four years together, I certainly do. They're a pack of designer-suited jackals.

Whenever my grouchy sweetheart of a boss goes down the coast for family events, he always comes back looking worn down by life and five years older. At this rate, he'll be a crumbly old man before I've hit thirty, and who wants that?

"I'll do it," I say. Never mind my bruised heart; I will rescue this buttoned-down grump from his nefarious relatives. "But I'm... you know..."

I wave a hand up and down my body. My boss's mouth twists, and his gaze rakes me from head to toe, cataloging my many flaws.

The crinkly, too-bright clothes, covered with a fine layer of cat hair; the bruise on my knee from roller derby. My messy hair that always escapes from whatever bun or braid I put it in. Take your pick.

Is he gonna change his mind? My fingers pluck at my purple skirt, and I swallow hard. Maybe he'll take it back and ask someone more suitable. Because let's be honest: if Sebastian wants to impress his snooty family, I'm the last girl in the world he should choose.

"No," Sebastian declares, stern eyes fixed on an ink stain on my cuff. "I need it to be you, Felicity. I'll coach you."

Oh, great. Learning all the ways I don't measure up for this man? Sounds like pure torture.

Because the Bamfords are old money. Country clubs and race horses and private vineyards—*that* kind of money. And I have raspberry streaks in my hair and a tattoo of my ancient cat Rusty on my wrist. My bus pass has seen more action than my credit card.

"Awesome," I say.

But as I slink out of his office, my bruised heart dragging along the carpet, I try to see the positive side.

And that is: a weekend event with my boss. Hours and hours together away from the office. A sneak peek at his origins, and the chance to give the evil eye to his awful relatives. Sounds fun.

And who knows? Maybe pretending to date me will open Sebastian's eyes! Maybe he'll scoop me over his shoulder like a bespectacled Tarzan and carry me into the sunset.

Yeah, right. Girls like me don't land dreamboats like this. We nurse our forbidden crushes, then go home alone and snuggle with our stinky old cats.

Hope Rusty is ready to be the little spoon when I get home. Today's been a doozy.

* * *

Check out Grump Gone Wild or read the whole series in the Grumps Unleashed box set!

xxx

Cassie Mint

About the Author

Cassie writes outrageous, OTT insta-love with tons of sugar and spice. She loves cookie dough, summer barbecues, and her gorgeous cat Missy.

You can connect with me on:
- https://www.authorcassiemint.com
- https://www.facebook.com/cassiemintauthor
- https://www.bookbub.com/authors/cassie-mint

Subscribe to my newsletter:
- https://www.authorcassiemint.com/newsletter